AWAKEN,
HANA

August 2016

AWAKEN, HANA

SALLY JO MESSERSMITH

Sally Jo Messersmith 챕2l

iUniverse®

May AWAKEN HANA become your prayer

AWAKEN, HANA

This is a work of fiction. All of the characters, names, incidents,
organizations, and dialogue in this novel are either the products
of the author's imagination or are used fictitiously.

iUniverse books may be ordered through booksellers or by contacting:

iUniverse
1663 Liberty Drive
Bloomington, IN 47403
www.iuniverse.com
1-800-Authors (1-800-288-4677)

ISBN: 978-1-4917-8125-8 (sc)
ISBN: 978-1-4917-8126-5 (e)

Library of Congress Control Number: 2015918081

Print information available on the last page.

iUniverse rev. date: 11/30/2015

Cousin Zola Payne, Grandma Minnie
Rudolph, and Zola's baby.

PROLOGUE

Hana

Could the day own a bluer sky? Or the sun shine with more brilliance?

Maybe the excitement in the faces of the gathering children was being reflected into the heavens. Soon, the time would be handed over to them and they would release the message to the world. They were hopeful and expectant. They believed that though their dreams would be carried to a place where dreams were suffocated, theirs would not be extinguished. The wind was strong this day and blowing in a northerly direction. The wind knew it had an important mission and even though these were children, what they held in their hands was powerful—powerful like a revolution. Words! The words were written on helium-filled balloons. One little girl's balloon had the single written word *Hana*.

Hana meant "one." It was a word of impossible hope. This little girl knew what she wanted. She spoke the word in a prayer. Others spoke different words out loud as the ceremony began. Someone said a prayer, and the signal was given to release the balloons. Dreams must be let go. They must be shared with others. Dreams can be more real than what we see in reality. In fact, reality starts with a dream. This little girl gave her prayer a little push and blew on it as she let it go. "Go, little balloon. Go quickly," she whispered. The wind picked it up like the others. The wind carried this *one* balloon higher. It carried all of them over the ugliest place, which stretched for miles. The children knew their words were stronger than the ugliest place. Now don't misunderstand; the ugliest place in the world had the beauty of trees, animals, and streams that stretched before them. It was ugly because it was built to separate. The little girl's balloon had a longer journey. Therefore, it touched down in the mountains before it crossed the ugliest place in the world. It had to pick up a seed before it crossed—a real seed from a real flower. The seed was slightly sticky and held fast to the balloon. The wind picked it back up again and carried it higher than all the others. It was crossing the country at an angelic speed. All the other balloons had already landed and had given their important dreams. However, it seemed like this balloon would leave the country altogether. It landed on the south side of a river. This river divided two countries. No one really lived here. Some people took walks along its banks, but it was against the law to cross. The seed knew it was time to let go. It fell into the soft soil. It died there, and then …

Dreams sometimes do the same. They are buried. They are like this seed in that they seem to be gone forever. But they are not. Someday they begin to wake up and grow again. Thousands upon thousands of dreams, spoken and unspoken, are buried in this soil, buried in the soil of this country. These dreams are spoken in prayers, released, buried, and then dreamed again.

This seed grew into an unusual flower. The stem grew and produced a wonderful flower. It was like the balloon that carried it there, white and puffed up with free air.

One flower.

The balloon that carried it had long since popped. The prayer "one," *Hana*, had not. It had become hidden in the beauty of this flower. The flower waited to dispense its miracle, which was assigned by the Creator Himself.

It kept waiting. It was for a miracle of *love*. And its beauty would be seen and enthroned in the heart of one who loved.

RUSSIA

Khabarovsk

Fuyuan

Harbin

Tumen River

Musan

NORTH KOREA

Pyongyang

Seoul

SOUTH KOREA

Beijing

CHINA

Ju's Journey

Kumming

LAOS

THAILAND

BangKok

CHAPTER ONE

THE BRIDE

She runs into his arms, and he enfolds her in his embrace. Her head falls gently against his chest. He feels strength enter him. Time is no more as they sense the essence of each other. He softly places his hand over her head and pulls her closer to his chest. The moment creates a crescendo of love for her. He strokes her soft ebony hair. She lets it loose from its hair ties. How long it is. How much he loves her! They hold each other in this timeless moment. His eyes close so as not to let it go. He opens his eyes and gently lifts her chin once their eyes meet. They look into the windows of their souls. Words are shared without either of them uttering a sound, yet they hold their meanings. She is a mystery to him. He feels her love for him and has no understanding of its reason or how it happened. He just accepts it. He feels thankful. But whom does he thank? Himself? Kim Il Sung, the "Dear Father"? This thought instantly makes his mouth fill with salty bitterness. Why? He had never felt bitterness before regarding the leader. He shakes his head slightly to bring himself back to her. It is best not to try to decide whom he should thank. He lifts her face to his and kisses her. He feels her love spread throughout his body. He is more than enraptured. Could it be she is possessing him? He wants her to become a part of him. He wants them to belong to each other in the most intimate way. They will marry within the day. He will wait. He pushes her away from him just a little. It helps diminish the surge of passion he feels so unbearably strongly.

They don't dare go beyond the first kiss. It is taboo. It is against the party. Purity is of utmost importance to the party. He has barely gotten permission to marry her. She is of a lower bloodline than his. Her family has been content to remain farmers, living close to Songnim. But this is what he loves about her. She seems unattached to the world around her. It is almost as if she doesn't belong to it. She is always happy. She always has something to look forward to. She especially loves flowers—wildflowers, in particular—even ones she has never seen. She helps him honor the party's stance on purity. There are times when he feels he can hardly contain himself.

"We must wait to have sex until after marriage," she tells him. She has told him their love for each other would be established because of their commitment to each other. If they took each other before marriage, they would be like flowers planted too early in the spring. The roots would be frozen and unable to grab the ground. Their love and admiration for each other could wither quickly. He might even grow to hate her. She said she had heard of it before and men had been known to leave their lovers before they were married. If she became pregnant, she would be forced to have an abortion.

"Trust me, Ju; if we wait until the marriage commitment, then we will have roots like the rock breakers that grow in the high mountains."

He trusts her and respects her. He swears it takes more strength than any man should have to have. This very moment, he feels it is cruel. He pushes her away from himself a little more.

"Tonight, Ju, tonight." She does the unthinkable and brings his hand between her breasts. "I love you. You are my home, and you are my one."

He takes her hand and places it on his chest. "I love you. You are my home, and you are my one." He breathes in deeply.

"Like the flower *doraji*. It is so full of joy it can almost burst; however, it waits ... one blossom. Like us, one blossom." She expresses herself as deeply as he breathes. He resists the desire to feel the soft curves beneath his fingers. He moves his hand from her breast and places it on her cheek.

"My doraji, my Sun'hi, my girl. I love your thoughts." He speaks her name like a sweet song. "I want to spend all my days with you and just listen to your thoughts. Tonight, Sun'hi, tonight."

She places her hand on his face in response to his unspoken direction.

"This time, you are the strong one." She smiles, her eyes downcast.

"Sun'hi, I am not strong. There are people who pass this way often." He shakes his head in response to her compliment. They hold hands and start walking along the pathway. His thoughts are all about her. He thinks of the day they first met and smiles to himself.

"You're smiling. What about?" she inquires.

"About you and the first day we met. What else is there to think about? You consume my thoughts, Sun'hi," he answers.

"I remember that day. My father and I had traveled from our village located near Songnim to reach Pyongyang, and it had taken an extra-long time to get there. The truck driver who gave people from our village a ride had run out of gas about three miles outside of the honored city. We had fresh vegetables. We had to get there soon and could not wait, so we traveled by foot." Sun'hi continues fondly, "It was a beautiful day. One I will long remember. My father and I sang songs and told each other stories. When we got into town, he told me to go to the nearby park to refresh myself at the little brook that runs through it while he set up the vegetables to sell. He cares more about me than himself," she explained.

"I notice how your father treasures you. He doesn't just appreciate you. He treasures you," he reflects.

"Oh, all fathers feel that way about their daughters."

"No, Sun'hi, they do not," he states vehemently. "Especially since he has no sons." He continues, "I have seen how he hugs you and kisses your forehead. He looks into your eyes, and I have heard him speak a blessing over you from the great father, Kim Il Sung. He affirms your value. And then you, you, you, Sun'hi, skip away like a butterfly, carefree." He confirms his statement. "On the day I first saw you, I watched you sit upon the rocks and put your feet in the stream. The sunlight sparkled on your hair. There were some boys playing football, and the ball got away from them and went into the creek. You took the time to get it for them. I haven't stopped thinking about you since."

"You, Ju, are crazy," she teases.

"I know, and it is all your fault." He gives her a gentle poke, and she runs from him. He soon catches her, and they find themselves in another embrace. "At this rate, we are never going to get to the courtyard in Musan," he says.

"I remember that moment," says Sun'hi.

"What moment?" His eyebrows wrinkle as he questions her.

"The first time I saw you, silly."

"Humph."

"You followed me from the park after you saved my book from falling into the water. You kept running into things!" She laughs.

"Yeah? Like what?"

"Like the little old lady carrying bags. You had to pick up all her belongings," she reminds him.

"Yeah, what else?" he challenges her.

"And the bush—you completely wiped out. I had left the brook and returned to my father's booth by the time you picked yourself up and approached my father. And then you tripped again. If you hadn't grabbed the table, you would have landed on your face. My father whispered in my ear, 'I think this young man has *fallen* for you. I sure hope it isn't for me.' I had to run away I was laughing so hard. And I have been laughing ever since."

"I'm going to get you now!"

Sun'hi runs away, and she is pretty quick. Ju takes off after her as she veers toward the wooded area. He catches her and twirls her around. She is still laughing.

"But my father, Ju, he was very impressed and grateful that you offered us a ride back to our village," she reassures him. "You have been such a great help to our family ever since." She guides him to a nearby rock, and they sit down.

"You know, Sun'hi, this was my home."

"I know, Ju." She squeezes his hand. "We will marry each other in town this evening under the moon. It will not be long, Ju." She hugs his arm and lays her head on his shoulder. "You love me, and I can hardly wait. Tell me about your home, your family here, Ju." She says his name with reassurance. "I want to know."

"My father used to bring us here for picnics. I wish you could have met him and my mother. But as you know, they have passed away. They starved to death. There was not enough food when I was a little boy. That is why they sent my brother and me away to my uncle and aunt in Pyongyang. They had no children, so we were allowed to go. I know they did not want us to go, but it was best for us." Ju looks far away into the distance, wondering at the passing of time. He doesn't cry or feel sorrow. The sorrow had faded a long time ago, along with his memories of his parents. "I was about ten years old when I moved away. Many of my classmates were starving, and some of them had died," he states matter-of-factly. The smell of the woods brings back the memory of his parents. He can see their faces in his mind. They become clearer as he continues to reflect. "We would fish here," he says suddenly, breaking the stillness of his thoughts. "My mother would make a campfire to cook the fish we had caught. They were simple people. They were faithful to the party; that is why they were able to get permission for my brother and me to leave. But they made me promise to return here when I married. I have respected their wish to come here and honor them. You know, Sun'hi, it is like they are here and want to meet you. I need to light a candle to honor their presence when we marry tonight in Musan. Oh, Sun'hi, I don't need to tell you all this. You know it already," he apologizes.

"Not so, Ju. I like it when you tell me about your parents. It helps me know you. And the sound of your voice is like the sound water makes when it falls over stones." She pauses. "Ju, your voice comforts me … Ju." She says his name again.

He closes his eyes as if he hears her voice in the center of his being. It is like he has come to know himself for the first time.

"Ju, I feel your voice inside my heart," Sun'hi says softly, as if she has heard his thoughts and made them her own. They get up from the rock and walk hand in hand in silence. They move closer to the river.

"It must be at flood stage," Ju informs her. "I can hear it roaring."

"Sounds a little out of control."

"It will be fun to go look at it."

"The roaring is drowning out the sound of your voice!" exclaims Sun'hi.

Ju barely hears her. Without understanding why, he finds himself falling. "Did I trip?" he wonders. He hits the ground hard. He is unable to move. *Am I being held? By what? Men?* He hears her screaming. "*Sun'hi*! Sun'hi!" he attempts to yell out to her. But nothing comes out. His breath has been knocked out of him. He attempts to free himself. He moves like the turbulent waters. He is like a man who has lost his reason. He swings his fists but hits nothing. He cannot see. He tries to open his eyes, but there is dirt in his eyes. And his mouth also fills with dirt. He tastes bitterness. Suddenly, his mind is dark.

CHAPTER TWO

STOLEN

Fear instantly grips Sun'hi like a vise. It grips her mind painfully. She hears screaming. The unearthly sound is outside of herself. Her voice is no longer hers. She feels the desire to rescue the girl she hears screaming, but she is helpless. Her captors push her to the ground. One of them has his foot on her back, holding her in place, taking all her power away from her. She instantly begins to pray to her Father God, but not with words, just her soul crying out in confusion and fear. She hears His voice speak to her.

"Open your eyes," He speaks in a voice only she can hear. She listens to Him, and in front of her eyes and within her reach is a flower—not just any flower but a *doraji*, the symbol of her love for Ju. Can it be real? Yet there it is: a dream come true. *How can a dream appear inside a nightmare?* she wonders. Before it escapes her, she grabs it quickly and places it inside her bra to press the unspoken words of hope against her heart. She knows God is with her, for it is a miracle. It transports her from this place of captivity. At that very moment, her hands are held behind her back. Lying there in the dirt, she waits, feeling the soft miracle push up against her breast. Her mind escapes her miracle. She waits for what she feels is inevitable. It never happens. They don't touch her, not one hair on her head. They force her into the back of a truck full of goods. She is aware of the truck backing up and pulling away. It drives over the uneven ground for a long time before finally driving onto a floating barge. She is keenly aware of water moving the truck up and down in a fluid motion and the swaying.

It can't be! Her thoughts race wildly. It can only mean one thing. *We are crossing water? We are crossing the Tumen River. I can hear it,* she thinks frantically. *No! No! No!* she screams inside herself. "Ju! Ju!" she screams. She knows she is being taken into China and leaving North Korea, her home. Somehow she knows she will never see her home again. Her eyes are shut. She closes them inwardly as well, searching for an answer, trying to escape the unknown. Then she remembers the flower. She retrieves it from inside her bra. She opens her eyes. She looks at it closely. *Can it be?* She cannot believe her eyes. A doraji is a single flower that grows on a single stem. "It is a gift from you, Father of Jesus." She begins to pray to God. "I thank you kindly. It is the flower I told Ju about—the flower of hope, the flower of dreams, the flower whose voice speaks the word *one*. One with Ju, one with you. But I did not tell Ju about you." She sighs. "I wanted to. But my father told me not to. He is a party member, you know. He doesn't know about you and me … He doesn't know how to know. Father …" She holds the flower close to her heart and continues, "Father, You are with me just like Grandma and Dad said You would be. I am so afraid. Don't let them touch me."

Sun'hi closes her eyes and feels Him cradling her. His presence begins to overwhelm her. She can feel Him smoothing her forehead, gently bringing her close to His breast. Her breathing slows, and she feels peace. She sighs, almost falling asleep. "Remember how Grandma called me 'Spring Joy'?"

Her thoughts float to the tender love of her grandma.

"Grandma?"

"Yes, my Spring Joy," she answers her in her thoughts.

"Tell me the poem about 'One' again."

"Hana, Hana, the name of the seed is sent on the wings of the wind. Singing the pure word to the foundations of all nations. No longer will hope be drowned. No longer will faith be imprisoned, and no longer will love be sold but given. The groom comes for His bride, uniting her to His endless embrace. The bride's prayer is answered. The nations bow. The kingdom comes. The flower is blooming. All of heaven sings the true name … Hana … *One*."

"Oh, that is beautiful, Grandma. I like to read, and you like to write. Why do you like to write?" she asks softly.

Her grandma sighs. "I suppose it is because my father, your great-grandfather, owned a printing press. It was how he made enough money to take care of all the children in our home." She continues with pride, "But I was his first. Do you remember how he adopted me?"

"Yes," she answers, "and how you lived through the war."

"Yes, you remember," Grandma answers sadly.

There are footsteps at the door. She rests her hand on the cool concrete wall. Before opening the door, she asks, "Is that you, Daddy?"

"Yes, it is." She opens the door for him, and he enters the dimly lit room. There is a small stove and a small kitchen table, along with a couch and a few throw rugs. He politely removes his shoes.

"Daddy!" Sun'hi runs and jumps into his arms. He playfully swings her around in a circle. "You have been gone forever, Daddy!"

"One minute away from you is too long," he agrees.

"It has been a long time, Koo Yang," says Grandma.

"It is good to see you, Mom." He gives her a hug. He is careful to close the door. "I wish I had more to bring to you. There is not much food available. The food rations are low. Kim Jung Il says we must learn to eat only two meals a day."

"Koo Yang, remember that he is not our provider. Jesus is," she states. "We are glad to have you. Besides, the garden is doing wonderfully, and we have enough to sell at the market."

Sun'hi interrupts. "Get the Father's Book, Daddy. Grandma and I waited all week to hear His words."

They wait silently in the front room, away from the only window in the two-room home while Koo Yang gets the precious book from the other room. Neither Sun'hi nor her grandmother know where it is hidden. The book's hiding place is kept secret to protect them if they were to be questioned. They risk their lives just owning it, let alone reading it or touching its adored pages. Before they read, they huddle close together in the center of the room on one of the throw rugs. Hanging over the couch in the proper place is a portrait of Kim Il Sung and Kim Jung Il. Sun'hi turns on the radio to the government station to conceal their voices. Koo Yang returns with the Father's Book. The pages have turned yellow with age and are smooth because of the loving hands that have touched them for the last sixty years.

"Daddy, we don't need Kim Jung Il's food anyways. We have God's food, just like Jesus, who said, 'Live by every Word that comes from the mouth of God!" she proclaims.

"Come here, Sun'hi. Sit close to me," Koo Yang directs. "What you say is true, and your words do encourage me, but you must be very careful not to criticize either the dear father, Kim Il Sung, or his son. Do you remember?" he sternly cautions.

"Yes, Daddy," she reassures him. "Out there, when I am thinking of Jesus, I say the Great Leaders' names, but Jesus knows I am talking about Him. I am careful."

Koo Yang holds his daughter close and then closer.

He thinks, *I can't protect her, but I know You can.* His eyes look heavenward. He speaks out loud, "We know the truth, and we have something others do not have. Even though we sit here in darkness, we have light. Even though we live like prisoners in our own land, we have freedom—freedom from sin. You do not have to pay for your grandfathers' sins in order to be cleansed, as they teach you in school. Jesus, the Son of the True Father of Glory, cleanses you of all your sin. Your mind has freedom; it has the freedom to choose to believe."

"And the freedom to feel His love," she adds. "I feel His love, Daddy." She turns to her Grandma. "Grandma, do you think others know Him?"

"They do," she answers encouragingly. "I remember when we did not have to hide," she continues. "I remember who they are; some of them are our neighbors." She lowers her voice almost to a whisper. "But it is dangerous for us to talk to each other. It has been many years with no end in sight."

"Daddy, the other day in school, I was singing a song to Kim Il Sung, but really I was singing it to Jesus. My friend nudged me and told me not to sing with so much joy or the teacher might suspect me. She gave me this look like she knew what I was really doing. I think she knows the Father of Glory," Sun'hi relates.

Koo Yang swallows hard and shuts his eyes. He thinks, *Why does my daughter have to live in a world where the very inflection of her voice can betray her?* "My little Spring Joy, I have taught you well," he praises her.

"Daddy, I know how to keep safe. Remember: I am not a child anymore. I understand your concern." She continues to reassure him. "Besides, Jesus really does protect me." She gives her dad a little reassuring peck on the cheek, looks him in the eyes. "I am fine."

"Tomorrow I'll take the vegetables to the market. There is truck leaving in the morning to take anyone in the village who has a license to sell."

"Please, let me go," she begs.

"You have school," he directs.

"Not tomorrow. It is our day off!" she answers with glee.

"Your grandma needs you," he refutes her.

"Koo Yang, let your daughter go. I'll be all right."

He gives in and sighs. "I would really like to take you. I could use the extra hand and the company."

"I love you!" she exclaims and wraps her arms around his neck.

"Okay, okay, okay, my young ladies." He winks at his mom. "Are there requests for tonight's reading?"

"Read John 17," requests Grandma. "Especially verse 11."

"I would be glad to." He begins to read, "'And I am no longer in the world, but these are still in the world, I am coming to You

Holy Father, keep in Your Name those whom You have given Me, that they may be one as We are One. While I was with …'" His voice fades away. Koo Yang would read long into the night before they would put the invaluable book and time away.

The following morning, Sun'hi and her father join the eager travelers headed to the capital. They all climb into the back of a large enclosed commercial truck. It isn't comfortable, as everyone must find his or her own space on the floor and a place for his or her goods. The day is good for travel on the paved highway. However, the truck breaks down about three miles outside of the city. They will have to walk. Sun'hi and her father don't mind, as it means more time to be together. Sales are good in the marketplace, and there is a park nearby that has a creek running through it. Sun'hi has brought along a schoolbook; concealed in its pages are poems her grandmother wrote that she wanted to read by the creek.

"Dad, is it okay if I take a walk by the creek?" she requests.

"I think that's a great idea. It was along walk today, and I think the rest will do you good." He urges her along.

She gives her father a kiss on the cheek. "I'll be back." She races to the coveted place where she can hear the rippling water dance over the rocks. The sunlight makes crystals of light join the water's afternoon frolic. She lays her cheek on a rock to feel the warmth of the sun but not for long. Soon she is up and skipping from rock to rock, defying the possibility of losing her balance and falling into the water. There really is no chance of that happening, as she has become a part of the syncopated rhythm of the water and light. She is living up to her name, Spring Joy. She finally sits herself down on a carefully chosen rock, one that can hold her comfortably while she reads, and the sun warms her cheeks. It is then that she notices him out of the corner of her eye. *Has he been watching me?* she asks herself. She acts as if he is not there. He watches her with his smiling eyes. How strong he seems to her—and tall. To her dismay, he walks over to her.

***

"Hello. My name is Ju," the young man offers.

Without looking up and in an attempt to discourage him, she responds coolly, "Was I asking for your name?"

He pays no attention to her demeanor, as he is running on nervous energy and has already planned what he is going to say next. "You like to read books and dance?"

Sun'hi does not answer him.

He sits slightly behind her on another rock, as there are no available rocks beside her. He senses she has no intention of answering his obvious question. He does not leave. He doesn't want to; she has captivated him. He wants to stay, not to annoy her but because he wants to be near her. It has taken every ounce of courage he had just to come over. Something about her makes him admire her.

***

Sun'hi is frozen on her perch. She feels the excitement from her head down to her toes. She wiggles them in an attempt to alleviate the feeling. It only seems to intensify it. He speaks again.

"My name is Ju, and I wondered if you would share with me what you are reading." He makes a second feeble attempt to engage her.

There is so much sincerity in his voice. She can't help herself and turns to look up at him, but he is behind her, causing her neck to tilt awkwardly backward. She hadn't realized he was so close. It upsets her balance, and she has to catch herself. In the process, she loses her hold on her book. Miraculously and to his credit, he catches it before it falls into the creek. She turns to face him, and her eyes meet his. She can see his sincere admiration. When he hands the book back to her, his hand touches hers. The excitement she feels now overwhelms and frightens her.

He asks, "Would you read something to me? Perhaps we could sit over here under the tree."

She nods. After all, he has just saved her book, along with her grandmother's poems. They sit under the tree, and she reads to him for what seems to be a long time. He listens to her, and their toes wiggle together as if the sunlight is playing with them.

"Do you mind if I read you a poem my grandmother wrote?" asks Sun'hi.

"I don't mind as long as you tell me your name," answers Ju.

"Sun'hi."

"Sun'hi." He repeats her name, and she can feel the warmth in his voice enfold her name as he seems to enfold her.

"I'll read you a poem about the stars."

After she reads the poem, he shares, "I know of a place where you can view the stars and understand their movements."

"I want to go to a place like that someday!" exclaims Sun'hi. "Have you been there?"

"I have. It is near the town I was born in."

Talking to each other becomes easy after this, and they lose track of time. So, much time passes, as if she were floating in a place where there was no time. And there they are, seven months later, on the night before they are to be married, looking at those very stars and in that very place. They are lying on their backs without speaking, just looking.

"Ju?" Sun'hi speaks.

"Yes, Sun'hi?"

"Ju." She repeats his name. She is loving him by saying his name. "I think sometimes when you look at the stars, others who are far away, like my grandma and my dad, are looking at the same stars, and even though they are not here with us …" She pauses. "They are with us. Here, let me show you." She gets up and moves to the other side of the wall. "Look at the stars again." She increases the volume of her voice. "Are you looking?"

"Yes, Sun'hi. I am also looking."

"See, we are together." She likes to tease him, especially since they are so close to being married. It really seems like tomorrow is forever and forever away and will never come.

"Maybe," answers Ju.

"Maybe what, Ju?"

"It is not quite the same as when you were right beside me. Would you come back?" he almost whines.

She takes the opportunity to tease him again. "Only if you can catch me!"

He jumps at the invitation, and it isn't long before he is holding her in his arms. It is what she really wants. He looks into her eyes. She can feel the oneness in them. He kisses her long and deep. She feels her entire being melt, absorbed by all he is.

"I love you, Sun'hi."

She turns around in his arms, and her back presses against his strong chest as she is enfolded. She tilts her head back to look into his eyes. She quickly turns back around. And in turn, she says to him, "I love you, Ju." She steps back a little ways from him. "Ju, look at the stars. We are together."

***

The cold wind blows through the walls of the truck. It wakes her up. And time returns.

Sun'hi looks up at the stars. Or has it? In that moment, she knows that Ju is also looking at the stars. She cannot feel his touch, his kiss, or his gaze. She is on the other side of the wall, and now miles separate them. She holds the flower close to her heart and presses it against her breast. She hears its song. She looks at the stars and feels the oneness of her and Ju and the oneness of her Father of Glory, who created her and Ju, along with the love they have for one another. She speaks the word *Hana*. It is a word of faith, of prophesy. It is a word that has faith in love. "Hana," she repeats the word again. It is a word that can move mountains. For it is stronger than what our eyes can see. "Hana," she says the word again. It is a true word. It is truth. "Hana, you mean *one* and nothing, nothing, will keep it from being true." She speaks into the cold darkness and lights up the sky.

15

CHAPTER THREE

A HUSBAND

The cold blast of air seeps into the truck again. Sun'hi has fallen asleep looking at the stars. She has hit her head on the inside of the truck. She has to grasp the side of the truck so when the road jolts the truck again, she will not hit her head. They have been traveling now for at least a day or two. If she were still in Korea, they would have already gone from one end to the other. The cold is bitter. No, *bitter* isn't a strong enough word. It is wrenching and seems to burn the outer layer of her skin, as the distance they are traveling from her home is burning her heart and seeking to destroy her.

Frozen fields surround a small building. This is where they stop. Inside the building, she is taken into a small room. She is told to sit down. An older Chinese man enters the room. He comes close to Sun'hi and looks under her hair. He tells her to walk across the room and back. He nods his head to regard her captors. They in turn take money from him. It seems to Sun'hi to be a large sum. Her captors tell her to go with the man. She belongs to him. She is now his bride. She has just been sold. They leave quickly before she knows she is being left behind. Her captors take with them any hope she has of returning to her home. Sun'hi starts to cry. She cries beyond her ability to stop. She has been kidnapped, betrayed, and now abandoned. Her new *husband* shakes her hard in an attempt to get her to stop crying. He pulls her toward the door. Once outside, he directs her by hand gestures that she is to get into his car. She does as he commands without thought. She is astonished to find two other women in the car with her. The other women's eyes are cast down, and they do not look up. The three travel for about two more hours. Always, they go farther north. They finally reach a small motel where they are taken into a room. An older woman comes into the room and bows to the three in greeting.

"I am Cheng. I welcome you to our village." She repeats this again in Korean. "I am here to prepare you for your weddings. You have each been given the honor to become a wife of a man in our village, Fu Yuan. I'll instruct you in the way of the ceremony, cooking Chinese food, and how to serve his manhood on your wedding night."

"Cheng," Sun'hi says respectfully, "I was brought here by force. I was to be the wife of another man the very day I was taken. I must be returned."

"Very well," answers Cheng. "But you must first pay the bride fee your husband has already given for you. When you return to your country, your government will consider you a traitor and put you in a prison camp. It is best for you to stay here and forget about Korea."

Sun'hi has nothing more to say, having lost her resolve with these words.

After three weeks of preparation, the day arrives for their weddings. They are each presented to their husbands. This is the first time they have seen them. Sun'hi can see her "husband" is much older than she. His hands are rough from hard work, and he is not particularly handsome. He seems boring. After the ceremony, he takes her to his home. Sun'hi does for him what she has been taught and submits to his desire. She cries out, as she is most uncomfortable and wants him to stop. She says nothing. She knows he will not stop at her request. She is only there for his pleasure. He does not care about her needs. He is as awkward and clumsy as he appears. She is his wife, and this is his right. She hears only his panting and feels his drool run down her neck as he pounds her insides like she is a dry water well, relentless and unforgiving, unaware of her presence and totally self-absorbed. She groans in pain. She endures this most unpleasant experience. She feels shame when he is done. His only act of kindness is to take her by the hand and show her the bathroom where she can shower. He shows her the kitchen and gestures to her that she must cook for him. He cannot speak Korean, but she has learned some Chinese and understands what he wants. His name is Zhao Tao.

"I will be gone for a few hours," Zhao Tao informs her. He lowers his eyes to her. "I am grateful to you. I am glad that you have become my wife. I will provide for you, and you must give me a son." He leaves her alone.

Sun'hi falls to the floor when he shuts the door. She does not speak to the Father of Glory. She is ashamed. She feels as if she has died. The Sun'hi she knows no longer exists. She feels she has become this man Zhao Tao's faithful dog. She can only breathe. She will have to function in her duties without hope, without joy, without love, without Ju, without her family and her homeland, and without God. The bitter cold of her environment and the distance from her homeland has frozen her heart. She slowly gets up off the floor. She walks back to the bedroom to put away the few things that are hers in the drawer he has provided for her. She sees her precious flower grown in her homeland. She looks at it blankly, unable to hear its voice of hope. Her ears are now deaf and her voice mute. However, out of respect to the flower and the Sun'hi who once lived, she carefully puts it away in the drawer as a memorial. Still, it is an act of faith, as small a gesture as it is, to keep it and not destroy it. It is a powerful act in the face of extreme devastation.

Sun'hi walks herself to the kitchen and methodically fixes dinner as she has been taught to do. Later her husband returns home. He is cheerful. He does feel love for her, but it is love like one would feel for a brand-new car or the excitement one might feel after winning a reward. He speaks to her.

"I am grateful you are here. I would have had no hope of having a wife. There are very few women available to men here in northern China. I hope you have made yourself comfortable. Have you put your things away where I have provided a place for them? Here, let me see?" Zhao Tao asks without waiting for an answer since she speaks very little Chinese. He walks into their bedroom and gestures for her to follow. She gets up from the dinner table to comply. He opens her drawer and finds her things neatly put away. He picks up her pair of pants, her shirt, and a few underclothes. "Is this all you have?" he inquires. "What is this? A flower? A dried flower?" He picks it up in his hands.

"Please?" she pleads in Chinese and then explains in Korean, "It has meaning to me." She holds out her hand for him to return it to her.

He hands it back to her and answers in Chinese, "I can't see harm in you keeping it. You are a peculiar girl. How did you manage to keep it this long way? And why? I think I'll call you 'girl with the flower.'" He shakes his head. "Peculiar."

Not understanding his words, she just nods, hoping that what he is saying to her is good. She puts the flower safely back in the drawer. He then takes her by the hand to the bed and insists that she meet his physical desires again. This time, after he is done with her, he falls asleep, as it is evening. The next morning, he leaves to work in the fields. It is hard work, and it doesn't pay much. It has taken all he has to buy himself a wife such as Sun'hi.

For Sun'hi, the meaningless days pass by uninterrupted. She looks at a gray sky even when the sun shines. Her ears only hear a dull, high-pitched sound that never ceases. Her own loneliness is her only companion in her unattached existence. This is how she survives in her bitterness and pain.

Soon Sun'hi is pregnant. She is almost certain after having missed four or five months of her menstrual cycle. She has also felt nauseous and very tired. She is most certain this is true when she feels the baby move. It is a fluttering at first. But it happens so often throughout the day she just knows it. The thought of having a child gives her an unfamiliar feeling—joy. This baby is her family, someone she can connect to. That night she has a dream. In her dream she sees her father. She runs to him and sits on his lap. "You came to me!" she exclaims. The dream is so vivid she can feel his arms holding her. The next morning when she awakens, she realizes she had been dreaming. Her husband, Zhao Tao, senses that she is despondent.

"Sun'hi, I think you need to get some sunshine. You never leave here. How about you go for a walk? If you walk straight down the street from the house, you will see a small park on your right. Most of the women who live here in the village go there to take their children to play. Maybe you will make a friend?"

Sun'hi understands her husband's words, but in her own silent protest at her situation, she refuses to speak the very little Chinese she knows to him. She nods her head in agreement. In an attempt to encourage her to go, he hands her a few coins.

"In the park sometimes there are vendors selling fruit or vegetables; buy yourself some. I insist you go. It has been a long winter, and it feels a little warmer today." She nods again and takes the coins he offers to her. He perceives her silence as acceptance of her marriage to him. He didn't marry her for her thoughts. He just wants her to stay healthy. He leaves for work as he does every day. Sun'hi decides to go for the walk her husband suggested. The village does seem like a pleasant place, and the sunshine invites her to keep walking. The dream about her father has made her feel happy, and the growing child inside her womb is like a gift from home.

Against her own will, she finds herself enjoying the moment. The park is not far from the house, and trees sway gently in the spring breeze. The buds on the trees give the whole place a lime-green appearance. She finds a creek running through the park. A large rock has settled itself on the other side of the creek. She walks behind it and finds a secret place. She knows it is a secret place because inside the small hollow place on the other side of the rock is a tiny makeshift child-size table, left by the occupant, who understands the value of secret places. She finds a comfortable place to sit inside and closes her eyes, allowing the sun's rays to soak into her skin and a dream to absorb her thoughts. She allows herself to be carried back to a hidden memory that had been pivotal to her pathway as a person.

***

"Sun'hi?" Her thoughts carry her to a moment as vivid as her dream had been the evening before.

"Yes, Daddy?" answers a very young Sun'hi.

"Come here. I want to show you something."

"Are we going for a walk?"

"Yes. A very long one. I have the day off, and as you know, I haven't had one of those for a very long time. I have packed us a picnic lunch. How about that? Would you like to spend the day with your daddy? I have something to show you."

"Yes! Yes! Yes!" Sun'hi jumps up and down along with her words.

And so they set off on the day's adventure, listening to the birds singing in the trees. It makes it seem as if the whole world wants to join them. It really is a great day with the sun shining and no clocks to tell them they have to leave. After a while, Sun'hi's legs grow tired, for it really has been a long way.

"Can you pick me up, Daddy?"

He picks her and she feels his strength and protection. He begins to whistle a tune. After a long while, they come to an abandoned building. Koo Yang pushes the door open.

"Daddy, how did you know this place was here?"

"Sun'hi, this is a very special place."

"What is that?" She points to an odd-looking table with some sort of rollers attached to a lever.

"This is a printing press. It prints newspapers, books, and poems. This was your great-grandfather's printing press—your grandma's dad."

"A printing press? What does it do?" she inquires with interest.

"It prints newspapers, books, and poems. This was where your grandma's poems were printed."

"Really? How does it print?"

"Well, this is the place you put the ink. Ink is like paint. The poem's words have to be set up with letters in this square box. Oh, look! There are a few letters left in the box." He hands them to her, and she holds them.

"They are hard. The letters are made out of metal, and they are backwards." She is perplexed.

"That is right. They are backwards so when they are printed on the paper, they look right to us. The ink is spread on top of the letters by these rollers, and the paper is set in this disk and brought down by these levers. Then the poem is printed on the paper. Do you understand?" he asks, thinking she does not understand.

"I think so," she answers. It is so foreign to her. "But why a printing press? Why would someone own one?"

"Well, it was a way to make money to buy food for his family. He would get paid for printing a newspaper and books. See, your great-grandfather was a minister of God. He was not a minister for a church but for orphans. He had many orphans, and your grandma was his first daughter."

"I remember the story; Grandma was left at the hospital by her birth father. And Grandpa was receiving treatment there for an injury and decided he would be her father. But why didn't her birth dad want her?"

"In the old religion, daughters are not always wanted, because they need a son to help the rest of the family to the next place when they die." He looked sad when he said this. "I have always wanted you, Sun'hi. I don't need a son to take our family to heaven. We have God's son, Jesus. He made you, and you are valuable to me. I am glad you are my little girl." He gives her a hug, and she smiles. She wipes the dust off the old printing press.

"I love this old place, Daddy. There must have been a lot of laughter here."

"Yes, there was. Let me show you something else." He walks into a hidden place in the wall. He then reappears.

"Where did you go, Daddy?" She giggles.

"Wouldn't you like to know? Here, take my hand. There is a hidden place behind the wall. A secret place. It was built during the war to hide food and young boys. Both could be taken by the Japanese army. I never experienced that for myself. I was born after the war. I used to come here and have a secret place all to myself. I would read books in here and talk to God. I was hidden from all the world. I felt safe in here. I could think and feel anything I wanted." Koo Yang looked pensive as he thought about his childhood.

"Daddy?"

"Yes, Sun'hi?"

"Didn't you tell me once that you never knew your father?"

"That's right."

"And I never knew my mother." She thought about this.

"We have each other and Grandma. It was Grandma who wanted me to bring you here. I think she wanted me to remember and for you to know where we came from. She wanted you to know the stories she has told you about the past were not just made up," he explained. The two of them explore the place the rest of the day. They eat lunch together in the secret place. While they are eating, Koo Yang tells Sun'hi something she will always remember.

"I just thought of something."

She nodded to let him know she was listening.

"God keeps us in a secret place: His heart. We can go there anytime and hide. He protects our hearts and minds there. He tells us the truth. When we go back home, maybe you will find a secret place of your own for you and God to share. He can hide you in this place. You can live there, and no one can take His home away from you."

***

23

Sun'hi opens her closed eyes in more ways than one. She looks around at her unwanted surroundings. "I haven't left my home, not my real home. You, Father of Glory, are my home. I can live in the secret place. You have given me a home no one can take from me. Thank You for opening my eyes," she says, not realizing she is speaking out loud to her forgotten friend.

"What did you say? Were you talking to me?" A young girl about her age speaks to her in Korean. Sun'hi sits up, startled to hear her language spoken out loud.

"No. Not me. I was talking to …" She pauses, looking around. "… to myself," answers Sun'hi.

"I understand. I used to talk a lot to myself when I first moved here. Hello, my name is Mi-Ran." Without waiting for a response, she continues, "Hey, you are the girl who married the old man Zhao Tao. You are her, aren't you? You have to be her. I wondered if you were ever going to come out of your hole. I am right? You are Zhao Tao's wife?"

"Yes, you are right. I am Zhao Tao's wife." Her tongue felt odd saying those words, "Zhao Tao's wife." Her face must have showed it.

"Did you just swallow a pickle?"

"No."

"What's your name?"

"Give me a chance, and I'll tell you!" She laughs. "My name is Sun'hi."

"Really? That was my great-aunt's name. She was funny."

"You are funny."

"Are you insulting me? You only get to insult me after you have known me for at least a day!" Mi-ran laughs.

"I didn't mean to insult you."

Mi-ran grins. "Don't worry. Where did you come from?"

"From just down the street."

"I mean in Korea."

"Korea?" repeats Sun'hi, as if she has never been there. After thinking for a moment, she answers, "A little village south of Songnim."

"I was from Chongjin."

"My fiancé was from Musan. Well, nearby there. We were going to get married." She looks down at the ground as she remembers a feeling she has not had in a very long time. "We loved each other very much …" She pauses. "I think."

"Sounds like a fairy tale to me. I am sorry; that was harsh. It is just no use thinking about boyfriends we have left behind."

Sun'hi gets up to leave. "Yes, like a fairy tale," she answers in a faraway voice. "Once upon a time," she whispers to herself.

"I am sorry. My mouth has no sensitivity." She puts her hand on Sun'hi's shoulder. "It has been a long time since I left home."

"You left willingly?"

"No, I was stolen. My friends and I paid for what we thought was a guide who could help us get to South Korea."

"You were escaping?"

"Yes, I was. But the guide took our money and sold us as brides, and here I am. All I can say is at least I am not hungry. Listen—I don't mean to sound so callous. I've just gotten used to living here. I have accepted the fact I am not going back."

"I could never do that, never."

"I remember feeling just like you. But something changed."

"What happened?"

Suddenly, a little boy, about three years old, runs up to her and sits on her lap.

"Mommy, do you have a cookie for me?" chimes the sweet little voice.

"Yes, Sang-Jin," answers his mother, Mi-ran.

"Who is that you are talking to?" He points at Sun'hi.

"Remember your manners," scolds Mi-ran.

"Oh, I forget." He bows his head. "My name is Sang-jin What is yours, miss?"

"Sun'hi." She gives the little boy a smile.

"Here's your cookie, Sang-jin."

"Thank you. May I go play?" He bows politely.

"Yes, you may." Mi-Ran gives her son a kiss. He jumps off her lap, and off he runs with some other children whose mothers have come to the park to spend the afternoon.

Mi-Ran finishes her sentence. "My son has made the difference. I am his mother, and I am not going to leave him. His father is kind to him and to me. I may not *love* him, but I do care about him."

Sun'hi decides at that moment to confide in her newfound friend. "Mi-Ran, I think I am pregnant. I am afraid. Can you help me?"

"I thought you were."

"You can tell?" Sun'hi is worried.

"Yes, you are showing, silly."

"I am." She fondly touches her stomach in a circular motion.

"To answer your first question, yes, I can tell you where to get help. Because you are not Chinese, you will not be allowed to go to the hospital. But there are some great midwives. I had one who came to my house. I can give you her name." Mi-ran pauses. "Have you told your husband?"

"No, not yet. I didn't know if I really was pregnant. I am sure I am now."

"I can see it."

The two young women repeat their discovery as to make it truer.

"You can?"

"Yes, I can."

"Do you think he can? My husband?" inquires Sun'hi.

"No, I think his eyesight is poor. The first thing you need to do is tell him. He can help you get the midwife I suggest."

Sun'hi looks downward.

Mi-ran gives her newfound friend a hug. "I know you may never love him. But you must learn to at least trust him. I can promise you one thing: you will love your baby, more than you can imagine. Can I walk you home?"

"Sure." She looks up and smiles.

"Congratulations! You are a mother."

"I am a mother." She gives Mi-Ran a hug. "I had no idea when I took a walk today I would come home with a friend."

Sun'hi has dinner ready for Zhao Tao when he comes home. He sits at the table while she serves him dinner.

"I must tell you something," she says. He looks up at her in surprise. He has not heard her speak during a meal since she came to his home.

"Please, go on. I am listening," he answers.

"I am going to have a baby."

He jumps up and startles her. She drops the pan of hot rice she is holding in her hand.

"This is good news!" he exclaims.

She sighs and continues, "I am going to need a midwife."

"Of course, of course. There is a local midwife who lives in town. I'll make an appointment for you tomorrow." He stops and looks at her with admiration. "I am so happy." He almost giggles with excitement.

CHAPTER FOUR

A BABY IS BORN

The growing child in her womb has made Sun'hi happy. The child has become her family, as small as he or she is. The child is her connection to the family she left behind. In the months that follow, she enjoys feeling the child move around. Sometimes he or she is very active. She wonders what he or she looks like and if he or she will look like her. Her arms sometimes ache to hold her child. She sings songs to him or her, mostly the song of her flower.

"Doraji, doraji, doraji! I walk over the pass where doraji flowers bloom." She gets the flower as she continues to sing. "It is a path that is familiar to me."

Zhao Tao walks into the room and watches her sing. "Are you singing to a flower?"

She does not answer him and continues singing to her child. "I look at these white flowers that remind me of my mother, in the evening with the twinkling star. Doraji, doraji, doraji. When I wear these white flowers on my hair, it reminds me of young days and my dreams." She carefully puts the flower away. Zhao Tao walks away shaking his head.

The baby makes her want to talk to her new friend, Mi-Ran. They take walks to the park together. They talk as they watch Sang-jin play. The midwife tells her she is healthy and so is the baby. The day is approaching when she will give birth.

The day starts as most of the days start, except this day, before Zhao Tao leaves for work, she is suddenly soaking wet.

She feels ashamed. She then realizes this is what it means when one's "water breaks."

"Zhao Tao, I believe my water has just broken."

"Your what?" he asks, and then seeing her for the first time this morning, he adds, "You are soaking wet!"

"I know. It means I could have the baby soon. I need you to get the midwife."

He quickly complies. He finds the midwife and brings her back to his home. He is no longer needed. He leaves cheerfully for work. Soon the contractions start. At first, they are far apart from each other. As the afternoon lingers, the midwife has her walk around, and they intensify, taking on a mind of their own. She is faithful to stay with Sun'hi. "The first baby always takes a long time," she assures her. She is still in labor when her husband returns home from work.

"She has not given birth yet?" Zhao Tao ask impatiently.

"She is young, and it is her first time. You must be patient," the midwife snaps back at Zhao Tao.

The sun has set when the contractions are finally strong enough for her to push. She lies down in the prepared bed and begins the process of pushing. The strength of the contractions overwhelms her. She begins to feel that it is impossible for her to go on, but her body gives her no choice. The midwife announces to her that the head has crowned, and with the next contraction, she must push. She pushes again and again with each endless contraction until she feels she has entered eternity. Zhao Tao watches and waits from the doorway. He is extremely nervous. Then it happens; the head is out, and with the next contraction, the birth is complete. The precious baby is laid on Sun'hi's bare chest, and they are both covered in a blanket. She feels glorious as the baby nestles in her arms. Her happiness is uncontainable. The midwife has safely cut the umbilical cord. The baby coos and sleeps in Sun'hi's arms. The midwife makes Zhao Tao leave. "Let the mother and baby rest together."

It isn't long before the baby wakes and is hungry, and the midwife helps Sun'hi nurse the baby. Afterward, Zhao Tao

29

is allowed to enter the room and hold his child. He holds the child and feels pride fill his heart as a long-awaited and expensive dream is fulfilled. He unwraps the child's blanket and is slapped with the realization that the baby is a girl. He yells from his gut and runs from the room and out the door with the baby in his arms. Sun'hi is left in shock. She does not understand what is happening. Hate begins to well up inside her for the first time. She begins to understand in her heart what is happening without asking. Her mind does not want to know. Speaking the unutterable words will force it to listen to something it does not want to hear. Tears of anger fall silently from her cheeks. She wants the anger and the hate to grow in strength so she can use it as a weapon.

The midwife begins to minister to the belabored body robbed of its reward. She washes her body, taking care of the afterbirth. She works without words or comfort. She seems almost indifferent. She has witnessed this happening many times. She herself feels helpless against the forces that condone this crime. Zhao Tao returns as abruptly as he had left without the baby. He pushes the midwife out of the way. He stands very close to the bed and leans over into Sun'hi's face. He states clearly in a whisper that screams in her ears, "Do not … *Do not* let this happen again. Deliver trash to me. You will give me a son!" He roars the word *son* so that it shakes Sun'hi. She doesn't have to ask him where her little baby girl is at; she knows without being told that he has destroyed her.

The midwife continues to dress Sun'hi and help her back into bed. Suddenly, Sun'hi feels such a surge of anger beyond her control she gets up and runs from the room and out the front door. She cannot think. Her feet know they must run to the secret place behind the rock. She can't get there fast enough. She throws herself on the little makeshift chair. She is cold and bleeding from the afterbirth. Her mind and body are near shock, and she is unable to cry. She just wants to escape. She closes her eyes, wanting to go to her Grandpa's printing shop.

Whether she falls into a deep sleep or passes out, it is hard to say. She awakens into her own dream.

"Spring Joy," she hears her grandmother's voice tenderly call her name.

"Yes, Grandma."

"Do you remember the story I told you about my father?"

"The story about your father? Yes, I do, but tell me again. I love to hear you talk."

"A long time ago, Korea was one. There were missionaries who came to our country. They were from the United States. One of these missionaries became like my second mother."

"Really, Grandma, I don't remember you telling me about her."

"I don't believe I have. Her name was Zola."

Sun'hi snuggles into her grandmother's arms. She knows it will be a long story. "Talk as long as you want. I love to hear the sound of your voice."

"Zola was a nurse. She was unmarried, and of course, she had no children. She worked in the missionary hospital in Pyongyang. One night, I was brought to the hospital with my mother by my father. My mother was very ill. I was only ten days old. She had blood poisoning. Something happened to her when she gave birth. They tried to save her life. But they were unable to do so. My father deserted me after my mother died.

"The missionaries at the hospital searched for my father. They were unable to find him. They searched for his family to no avail. My extended family did not want me. They felt since my mother had died, there was no chance for the family to have a son."

"Why? Grandmother, why would anyone not want you?" inquires Sun'hi.

"The old Shinto religion requires sons to help them go to heaven. They need them to meet with the ancestors and ask for forgiveness and guidance."

Sun'hi snuggles in closer to her grandmother, not wanting to let go.

"After being abandoned, there was no place to take me. Zola took care of me for many months. She would take me home with her at night to her room at the missionary dorms and bring me to the hospital during the day. Zola was my second mother. However, a little girl can't grow up in a hospital. Zola prayed for a family to take care of me. Soon her prayers for me were answered.

"One night, a man was taken to the hospital with appendicitis. He was very sick. He was also full of broken needles that had broken off near his spine. He had gone for help for his appendicitis to a sorceress from the old religion. They had pushed the needles into his body to make the devils leave. He came to the hospital out of desperation. The doctors were not sure what to do. They treated him with medicine and surgery, and they prayed to the Father of Glory to heal this man. He miraculously recovered.

"The man was so grateful. He knew this was a miracle. He felt he had been touched and healed by the Son of Glory, Jesus. He believed Jesus was the one true Son of God and that He could save his soul. He said, 'Jesus is the only firstborn Son who can guide him and his family to heaven.'"

As this man recovered, he learned about me, how my mother had died and I had been abandoned by my father. He would hold me and feed me, tell me stories, and take me outside for walks. When it was time for him to leave the hospital, he did not want to leave me. Even though I was a little girl, he valued me. He wanted to be my dad and give me a home. He said it would break his heart to leave me. I became his daughter. He was a great dad."

"He was my great-grandfather." Sun'hi's heart smiles.

"Yes, child. He was your great-grandfather. Now, hush and listen. He wanted to open a nursery to help poor working mothers in the countryside. The church didn't know how to help him. The Lord was the one who gave him the clever idea of developing a business that would support the nursery—a printing press. It worked. No one had heard of such a way to help the poor before. Most help had come from donations. The business thrived. My dad was a minister to many children.

"Wonderful days followed as I grew under his watchful care. I began to write poems, and he began to print them. Then I learned how to use the printing press, and I printed my own poems. Zola would come by when she had a few days off. She was amazing to me because she had been to places I had never been, like Japan and China. My favorite story she told me was about Chide, a high mountainous range in southern Korea. She told me about the flowers that grew in abundance. She had brought some back pressed in a book. I drew pictures of them. I became quite good at it.

"But there was a dark cloud looming over these happy days. Zola would talk to my daddy about the encroachment of Communism from the north. Zola had also traveled in northern Korea where the Russian Communists were doing unspeakable things. She said they were teaching the Koreans in the north not to support the people from the USA. She said they were subtle and they were good at spreading their lies. They stated the Americans supported the Japanese controlling our country.

"When I was ten years old, Zola had to leave; she was not well and had to go back to the USA. I understood that she and other missionaries had given us a great gift, Jesus, the Son of God. I knew they were not evil. How could they be? They had given me care when no one else would and had given my father's life back to him. They were respectful and kind. Many Koreans had become Christians, and they were pastors and leaders of their own churches.

"During World War II, the hiding places were needed to hide young men while the Japanese occupied the land. Our building that housed our printing press became a perfect place to hide these young men. I had fallen in love with one of these young men and married him. He was your grandfather.

"After the war, the Japanese left our land, and they were replaced by another kind of evil, Communism—the evil Zola had spoken of to my father. World War II had ended. However, the battle for Korea had only just begun.

"My dear husband fought for freedom. He fought with South Korea and the United States to stop Communism. He wanted to free all of Korea. The thirty-eighth parallel became the line that split the country. Our family lived in the north, the wrong side for freedom fighters. He was made a prisoner of war, and I have not seen him since."

"I have never seen him." Sun'hi sighs.

"No, Daughter, you have not." Sun'hi's grandmother caresses her cheek. "He did leave me with a son, your father. It was only the two of us. We were a family. We would hide in the hiding place at the printing press building. We would worship the Father of Glory and read His book. He, the Father of Glory, became our hiding place, our secret place. I want you to understand something; this secret place God has made available for us is not a building."

"It's not?" Sun'hi speaks dreamily, not wanting the moment to pass.

"No, dear, it is not. The building that holds the printing press is not close by. We had to move away. The place where God hides us is always close by. Your real life is hidden with Christ in God. I was a baby when I was thrown away like trash and abandoned, but a brave man became my father. It is wrong to throw children away. It was wrong for my first family to throw me away. But my Father in heaven, He loved the very people who would do these terrible things. He taught me to love them too. He wanted me to be strong and to have the strongest weapon, forgiveness. This doesn't mean we condone evil. Love does hate evil and injustice. Do what you have to do to fight injustice even if it means risking your life. The Lord will always hide you in His love and hide your heart in His love. He will make you strong so you can love those who do not know how to love."

Sun'hi sits up and looks into her Grandma's face. "I will. I will. The next baby girl I have, I will hide her. I will be like your father and hide her with my love. I will use my anger to fight injustice. I will be strong and brave. I will forgive Zhao Tao. Forgiveness will be my weapon. Grandma, I love you. I love you!" Her own voice fades away, as does the vision. She feels the cold gripping her body like a vise. Hearing a familiar voice makes her stir.

"Who are you talking to?" Mi-Ran comes from behind Sun'hi, who is passed out on the ground. She reaches out to touch Sun'hi's back. "Is someone else here?"

Sun'hi looks around for her Grandma, a little disoriented, and then she realizes where she has fallen. "It is only me," she answers weakly.

"I thought I would find you here. You need to get back home. You'll die here. You already feel like death."

"Oh, Mi-Ran, he took my baby. She was beautiful."

"I know he did." She sighs.

"He took my baby!" She begins to cry deeply.

Mi-Ran holds her, trying to get her to stand up.

"Sun'hi, we can't stay here. You need to go home where it is warm. You must come with me. I'll stay with you all night. You must come now!" she commands her friend.

Sun'hi painfully gets up, not realizing how dizzy she has become. Mi-Ran manages to support her. She gets her home. The midwife has sent Zhao Tao away and bathes Sun'hi in a warm bath with healing herbs. She tenderly washes each arm of the dirt and pain. She washes her hair. As warmth and life returns to her body, Mi-ran combs the tangles from her friend's hair. Tears fall from her eyes as she shares her friend's grief. She is helpless to rectify the crime committed against her friend. Together, Mi-Ran and the midwife get Sun'hi into bed. They cover her in warm blankets. Mi-Ran lies next to her friend and holds her all night. They weep silently together. They do not speak about the baby girl again. It is too painful.

Chapter Five

IF YOU WERE A BOY

In a few weeks, Sun'hi is expected to return to her life as normal. She forgives the man known as her husband as best she can. She is his servant and nothing more. It isn't long before she is pregnant again. This time, Sun'hi resolves to keep her baby alive. She is not sure how she will do this. The answer comes from a most unusual source, her own husband. Just a few weeks before she is to deliver, her husband gets a job as a logger. It is in Khabarovsk, Russia. It will be his job to transport lumber from the forest to the Chinese sawmills near Khabarovsk. The job will pay very well but will keep him away from home for months at a time. He will not be home when she gives birth, and when he does come home, it will be for only a few days. He leaves with the promise to return.

"Good-bye, Sun'hi." He pats her on top of her head. "You are a good wife, Strange Girl with a Flower." This is his term of endearment for her. He is happy about making more money and returning home to a newborn son. "You must call our son Zhao Yen."

It is a few weeks later when Sun'hi gives birth. The midwife comes to attend to her. The baby is healthy, and Sun'hi feels joy return to her. The little baby girl is her family. She is bright, and her eyes search for her mother's face. Gazing into her eyes, she coos, "Little one, I must hide you. My daughter, if you were a boy, I would call you Zhao Yen. If you were a boy …"

She says it again as if she has discovered something. "If you were a boy! I will hide you as a boy! Your name is Zhao Yen."

Little Zhao Yen is dressed as a boy. It will be close to a year before *his* father returns to see him for the first time and only for a short visit. Sun'hi has told no one of her plan. If she hides her from her husband, she must hide her from everyone, even her friend Mi-Ran.

When Zhao Tao returns, he is so happy to have his son, Zhao Yen. He plays with him and feels so much pride as a father. Sun'hi is careful to always take care of Zhao Yen's physical needs, bathing him in the morning before his father wakes. Zhao Tao's visits are brief, and his mind is as dull as his eyes. This helps to keep Zhao Yen's true identity hidden. This arrangement goes on for about four years. However, there is an approaching event that fills Sun'hi with dread. This is when the little boys go with their fathers to a sauna alone. A ceremony happens at this time. It is a local tradition. Most likely, Zhao Tao will discover Zhao Yen is not a son but a daughter. The questions race through her mind. Will Zhao Tao dispose of his child? Will they both be sent back to Korea? Sun'hi knows half-Korean children are not accepted there. Could it be possible that he has fallen in love with his own child and would continue to love Zhao Yen as his daughter? Sun'hi has no plan.

It is Zhao Yen's fifth birthday, and Sun'hi has promised to take him to the large marketplace just outside the village. The railway station is there, and it is an exciting place. People seem to come from everywhere—musicians, acrobats, magicians, artists, dog trainers, and food vendors. The sights and smells could take away the worries from even the most troubled soul. Zhao Yen has a thousand questions for her mother, and not all of them can be answered. She feels herself enjoying her child. It is a good activity, and she is glad to have brought her. While watching a dog show, from behind her, she hears a voice she recognizes.

"Girl with a strange flower?"

The voice startles her. It is familiar but not Zhao Tao's.

"Sun'hi?" She closes her eyes and grips the hand of her son, frozen in her tracks. She hears the voice again. It must be the voice of an angel. "Sun'hi, open your eyes." The voice trembles, and it's owner is now standing in front of her. "Open your eyes, Sun'hi. It is me." She opens her eyes, and there before her stands her Ju. *Inconceivable.* She gasps, for she is looking into the eyes of her miracle.

CHAPTER SIX

LOOK INTO THE EYES OF MY BELOVED

Ju looks into the eyes of his beloved. He suddenly feels weak as an overwhelming feeling of love floods his empty heart. He has lived the years without her numb. His whole body shakes as he feels life spring back into his being. He feels darkness as strong as death lift off his core. He had been unaware of the gripping darkness and how it had infiltrated his mind. He felt as if he had been buried alive the day he had lost her.

At that very moment, as he beholds her, his mind transports him to the dreadful day. It has become so real he can still taste the bitter dirt in his mouth. He can hear the sound of those voices as if he had just woken up from the blow to his head. They are the voices of the men he had spoken to the day before they had arrived in his hometown, Musan. They were businessmen who took goods from Korea to sell in China. They had asked about Sun'hi. He had informed them how she was his fiancée and they were to be married the next day. It is then he realizes he had been betrayed or he unknowingly had betrayed Sun'hi. They had stolen her and taken her into China. For what? Would they bring her back? All his thoughts are unanswered questions. He tells himself, "I should have told them she was my wife. They would have left her alone. Idiot!" he berates himself. "Why did I talk to them about her? Where did they come from? It was like they were looking for me." He tries to stand up, but he falls instantly to his knees. His head had been hit hard, and standing up causes him to reel. He pulls himself up, using the trunk of a tree and holding on to it to regain his balance. He is disoriented. He has no idea where to go or what to do. He walks to his truck and drives to the home that had once belonged to his parents and his grandparents.

This was why he had brought Sun'hi so far from her home. He had not come to his childhood home for a very long time. His parents had sent him and his brother away to live with his uncle and receive an education. They hoped their sons would be accepted as party members. Ju's parents had remained. Ju knew when he left he would never see them again. The real reason they were sent away was to escape the severe famine that had gripped the area. People, especially children, were dying by the thousands. His parents were deemed loyal to the party and were allowed to send their sons away for education. But the real reason was to save their lives. The education was secondary. His parents would not be able to save themselves. They were grateful to the party who allowed them to help their sons. They worshipped Kim Il Sung and Kim Jung Il. They would live on in their sons.

After managing to walk into what almost seems like a ghost town, he asks a few remaining residents some questions and he is able to relocate his childhood home. The home has remained unoccupied. He pushes open the door of the humble home, which is not much more than a hollow cement block. Hanging on the wall in its proper place is a picture of Kim Il Sung and Kim Jung Il. He is looking at it with the proper respect he has been taught when he becomes keenly aware of the dirt still caught in his mouth. Without thinking, he spits it out on the floor in front of the picture. It wasn't on purpose; it was just a reaction—or was it? He looks around the abandoned room and finds, lying on a makeshift shelf, a book written about Kim Il Sung and his son Kim Jung Il. He picks it up and flips through the pages. Out falls a small piece of paper dated 1934. Written on it are instructions not to support the United States. The foul country would destroy Korea's independence, causing the chosen people shamefully to rely on them. He feels a sense of pride that his family was supportive of the party. His mother had been elected by the *inminban* (neighbors, people groups) to keep tabs on the neighborhood. This was a great honor, and she received respect from all who lived in the neighborhood. Living so close to Russia had given them the advantage of receiving the truth, unlike the South Koreans, who lived in shame. He feels gratitude to his parents who thought more highly of the party than themselves and had been willing to send his brother and himself away to improve them for their country. It had also saved their lives. He investigates the book a little further. Flipping through the pages, he discovers a small pamphlet cleverly hidden inside the binding. Written on the front are the words, "Life of Christ." On the inside of the pamphlet, he finds his mother's name handwritten. This is perplexing. He decides to tuck it back into its hiding place. He puts the small book in his pocket.

"Mom, I miss you," he says out loud. He remembers how she had managed to get him a special treat for his birthday before he had left. The whole family used to take walks to the river. His dad taught his brother and him how to fish. Their mom would grill the fish on a small campfire. Thinking of this cheers him. They were nearly forgotten memories. Once his father had taken him to the place built thousands of years ago to study the stars. He had just taken Sun'hi there the day before. He decides to go there again. By the time he arrives, it is dusk and the first stars are appearing in the sky. He looks up. Could she be looking at the same stars? Just on the other side of the wall? He runs around the wall but finds only loneliness and regret. He feels ashamed at his inability to protect her. Hopelessness overwhelms him. He wants to escape—somehow. He remembers passing a local bar on his way to the observatory. A few drinks might help to numb the pain. Inside the dimly lit room, he finds his brother. In the midst of the confusion, he has all but forgotten about his brother.

41

"Where have you been, Yoo Sang-jun? I could have used your help! I was attacked, and Sun'hi was stolen by those traveling businessmen who spoke to me yesterday!" Ju cries angrily at his brother.

His brother does not answer.

"Where were you?" Ju demands again.

"I have been looking after you," he answers with equal anger.

"How? I haven't seen you since we talked to those evil men."

"I have rescued you, Ju, my brother."

"What are you talking about?"

"I arranged for Sun'hi to be sold to those merchants as a bride to some Chinese farmer. She is gone from you forever."

Before Ju could think, all the anger, confusion, and bitterness came out in a powerful blow to his brother's face, knocking him off his chair and halfway across the room. Ju is on top of him as fast as he had hit him. He pushes his foot hard into his brother's face.

"Let me up now, Ju!" Yoo Sang-jun retaliates and grips Ju's foot. He twists Ju around, landing Ju facedown on the ground. Holding Ju firmly in place and giving him no room to struggle, he says, "You must finish listening to what I have to say. You would have ruined us if you had married Sun'hi."

Ju's silence fills the air with unbridled anger.

Yoo Sang-jun shakes him hard. "You idiot, she was sent to destroy you."

"How?" Ju grits his teeth.

"I investigated her background, and she is of the hostile class. Her grandfather fought for South Korea and was taken prisoner. Her family is a disgrace, and you know as well as anyone you would have lost everything you have gained by marrying her. You would have lost everything our parents died for to give us a chance at a better life. Maybe that is okay for you, but it is not for me. Your actions would have dragged me down right along with you. I am sure she was some kind of witch and cursed your mind with blindness. I sold her for a good price to the businessmen. I told them of your whereabouts, and they took over from there. She doesn't love you."

Ju's anger weakens. He feels betrayed by something unseen that he cannot understand. He feels defeat press heavily on his shoulders. His brother relaxes his hold on him.

"You'll be back to work on time in two days."

"I'll be back to work, Yoo Sang-jun."

Yoo Sang-jun gives his brother a hand to get him back on his feet. "There should not be a love greater than the love you should have for Kim Il Sung and Kim Jung Il."

Ju nods his head in agreement.

He leaves the bar. Outside, he looks up at the sky. The sun has set, and dark is approaching fast. He says out loud to no one, "But I love her." He decides to walk back to the old observatory. He wants to view the stars. Somehow, he feels he might find her there and ask her why. He walks to the ancient place. He feels a sense of reverence. The place is thousands of years old. He touches its ancient walls and looks up. The night is clear, and the stars are brilliant. He feels that Sun'hi is looking at the very same stars. It makes him feel loved. He hopes she feels loved. He looks up for a long time, not wanting to lose the moment. He thinks about the night before, how they could be far away and look at the stars and yet be together. Did she know they would lose each other? He decides to run around the wall where he had found her the night before. But all he finds is loneliness and regret. He has taken his eyes off the stars, and the moment has been broken. Love will do him no good. It will only fill him with hopelessness. He must return to work and become a machine. He must become hardened. However, the love he had received from Sun'hi would not fade away, though it may be hidden. It could not be conquered by hardness. It had not come from himself. It had come from beyond himself. It was indestructible.

Back to work.

***

Ju stands close to the rigging he is overseeing. It had seemed as if he had never left. Working hard every day and with intense dedication had earned him a promotion. The confusion he had felt had turned to anger. The line of work he is in has given him the opportunity to defuse it daily. He has an unending supply of anger. It makes him relentless, which helps him at work. Every day, he goes home to his small, one-room apartment. He sleeps there. One unlucky day, he is given time off. He finds himself walking in an area of Pyongyang, known as the Black Market District. He has no plan and does not really know why he decided to buy a radio. It has been rewired so it can receive forbidden radio signals from South Korea. It is absolutely forbidden to own one, and if discovered, it would be a fast ticket to a gulag{Korean labor camp}. The radio Ju had bought is small enough for him to hide safely in his backpack. When he gets home, he conceals it safely inside the mattress pad of his bed. He already owns a government-approved radio tuned to the correct signals. He decides the safest way to listen to his new radio is to have the old one on at the same time. When he is at home, he has it playing constantly. It drowns out the silence. The new radio he only listens to when he lies down to go to sleep. He sets the volume as low as it can go and holds it close to his ear. He isn't sure why he bought it or why he is listening to it. Something inside him wants to know something different. His first interest is music. It is so different, exciting, and soulful. However, some of it is loud and angry. It grips him. He becomes addicted.

He begins to listen to a signal hosted by individuals who had once lived in North Korea. They talk about a network of people who help people escaping North Korea. *Why would anyone want to leave, especially to a shameful place like South Korea?* he wonders. He has no plans of ever leaving. He does what he is told. It is easier that way. He doesn't have to think. He doesn't have to make choices or plan. He is part of a great machine that works for the good of all. He is a machine. So why the radio? He doesn't attempt to answer the question.

The party members who observe the neighborhoods believe Ju is unquestionably dedicated. It is no surprise when he is called to the vacation villa of Kim Jong Eun, the supreme and divinely appointed leader of North Korea, in Chongjin. Ju had been told to evaluate the place where a wooden floor was to be built inside a personal gymnasium for the leader. Ju had been noted for his expert knowledge of the variety of grains of wood. He also had already made numerous trips to the Korean lumber camps in Russia. He would transport men to the train stations or travel to as far away as Khabarovsk to acquire wood for special projects. This new assignment commissions him to Khabarovsk, Russia, to personally handpick the wood that will be used for the floor, the finest wood in all of Russia. The leader wants Korean pine nut for his precious floor instead of the transitional maple used for basketball courts. It is known there are Chinese sawmills in the area that cut the wood correctly. They are selling what is considered illegally forested wood to the United States. He expects to be gone for a few months. As he had already made the journey a few times and had obviously returned and in a timely manner, he is trusted. He is also skilled. This is why he finds himself in the villa of the leader. He actually feels excited. He, along with a few others, who would work under him, are going to meet an American who had befriended Kim Jong Eun. He is a famous basketball player. It seems strange to Ju that the divine leader would make himself available to an American. But it is no stranger than him wanting to listen to a radio that broadcasted foreign ideas. It just shows the leader's generous nature to invite someone into his presence who was deprived of the opportunity to be part of the Chosen.

The American is shown where the construction is to take place. Ju, along with his team, are taken by surprise when Kim Jong Eun, along with the American, enter the site. They all quickly stand at attention with their hats off and their heads bowed. They had seen pictures of the American before and know he is of African descent. It still takes them aback to see how tall he is. They don't dare look up unless addressed—except for Ju. He looks up slightly when the massive man walks by and catches his eyes briefly. They are asked to relax, and as a group, they all look up.

The American is introduced, and he shakes all their hands, as is the custom. When he shakes Ju's hand, he hands him a calling card with a picture of a flower on it and says very clearly in Korean, "Look." No one seems to notice the secretive gesture, except for the startled man making the transaction.

***

Earlier that week, before the American had flown to North Korea to visit with his friend, the infamous world leader, he had been approached by his grandmother. She was angry with him.

"Are you aware, young man, that you are friends with a man who treats his people like slaves? And yet you say nothing. Are you even listening to me?"

He knew better than to contradict her. As small as she was, she stood at least a good foot higher than he when she spoke. "I was praying for your sorry soul last night, and I am not certain why, but the Lord told me to hand you this picture of this flower. It was given to me by a Korean friend who told me all about Korea, firsthand. The flower loosely means 'one' or 'oneness.' I was told to tell you to hand this card to the Korean who looks up and say the word that means 'look.' I know this a strange request and far-fetched, but it has something to do with freedom. Our people should be about freedom," she scolded her grandson.

He knew disobeying her might be worse than disobeying God Himself.

***

Ju doesn't have a chance to look at what he has been handed until he gets home. When he looks at the small card, he sees a picture of a doraji, the flower Sun'hi had talked about when they were together. He had not thought about her until then. She had vaporized from his mind. The thought of her brings back something hidden from him for these last five years, love. The lingering word *look* was like a command, but from whom? The American had looked more perplexed than he felt.

Soon the day when he is to travel to Russia arrives. He had been listening to his illegal radio the evening before. He heard a song that had the word *hana*, meaning "one." He feels strangely awakened. The light from the dawning sun barely illuminates the room—a little like his mind. He had decided to pack the family book he had found in his parents' home a few years before. He is also bringing with him his savings, which is a good amount because he spends almost nothing and his job affords him the opportunity to make money outside of his ration paycheck.

It is time to leave and pick up the crew of men who would be waiting for him at the train station. The long trip to Russia is always unpleasant. It isn't the first time he has transported eager men to the lumber site. It is an opportunity for them to make more money for their families. This never happens, and they have to learn not to dream. Most of them would never return; they would just die. This small crew would return with him. Still they would be gone for a few months.

Once they arrive in Khabarvosk, Ju frequents the only place a foreman can sit and relax, which is a bar. Inside, it is fairly warm. Dinner is served, and as a foreman, he is treated with respect. Ju feels a little like a king. He sits back in a chair quietly when he hears someone speaking Korean or what sounds a little like Korean. There are newcomers to the site, Chinese farmers who have been offered the opportunity to come to Russia and work the lumber camps. They are about the only group in China who view this as an opportunity. He is aware of the newcomers, but it takes him by surprise to hear a few words in his own language spoken by this individual in a broken way. He decides to approach him.

"Hello?" he says to a man in Korean. "Would you mind if I bought you a drink?"

The farmer turns around, surprised he has been understood.

"It would be nice to speak to someone who speaks my language."

"Well, only a little."

"Enough for me." Ju sits down. "How long have you been here?"

"I've been coming to Russia for about 5 years. I've been in this part of Russia for about 9 months," the man answers.

"My name is Ju."

"Zhao Tao."

"Zhao Tao, I am here on commission to acquire the finest precut Korean pine nut Russia has to offer. You wouldn't happen to know someone who could point me in the right direction?"

"You are looking at him. I work for a sawmill that cuts wood delivered from the logging camps in the far north. I happen to be on my way there to pick up a load of logs to bring back to the sawmill. I assume you have a truck?"

"Yes, and a very small work crew. I also have a with me a man who is capable of driving like myself."

"I am leaving in the morning. You are welcome to follow me. Maybe we could help each other out."

"Certainly. I can't believe my good fortune. I was told I might be able to find a contact in this place. But I didn't think I would find someone this quickly. May I buy you a drink?"

"I would appreciate it. I thought most Koreans were dumb—I mean mute—but you seem to be different."

"Thank you for the compliment, I think. By the way, how did you come to speak Korean if most of us are so dumb?"

"My wife, she came from Korea. I bought her as a bride about five years ago. Peculiar girl, well, that is what I call her—'Peculiar Girl with a Flower.' She is a good woman. She gave birth to my son about five years ago."

Ju is taken aback by this description of his wife. "I am curious why you call her Peculiar Girl with a Flower."

"The first night we were together, she had this pressed flower she kept like it was gold. I let her keep it. I just thought it was peculiar. She even sings to it."

"Is it a white flower that looks a little like a balloon?"

"It's just a Chinese bellflower. Nothing special."

They talk for a good long while. During the many nights that follow, they talk. They work hard together as a team, acquiring the logs they need to bring back to the sawmill. They both have their assigned quotas. Working together makes their assignments easier, and they are done sooner than their required time. This gives Zhao Tao some unexpected time off, enough to return home briefly. He and Ju have become good friends, so he invites Ju to his house for a visit.

"Would you like to come visit my home?"

"I guess I could come with you. I have about three weeks before I return to Korea. I could visit. I am allowed to travel though China if need be. I could come for about a week."

"Perfect. My son and I will be part of a ceremony held at the local sauna. This event is for our sons after they have turned five. You have become a good friend, and we have worked together. I am able to return home for a short time. I did not think this would be possible until next year."

"So, what is the plan?"

"I will have to leave with my fellow crew members. And you would have to take the train."

"I'll meet you at the train station near your home."

"The train station will give you directions to my home. It is within walking distance. You can meet my son."

"Yes," he said and thought to himself, *And the Peculiar Girl with the Flower.* He had been careful not to mention his wife again. Could it be Sun'hi? It was a hope against all hope, but he had to go see. *I was told to look,* he said to himself. "I could be your son's uncle; I'll bring him a present," he answered Zhao Tao.

***

49

Ju arrived in Fu Yuan before his friend, and there he stood before Sun'hi. Did his own eyes betray him? She had to be an illusion.

"Sun'hi, I was told to look for you and I found you."

"How, Ju? How did you find me?"

"I was told to look." He handed her the picture of the flower. "It's the flower you told me about so long ago. A man gave this to me and told me to look. I knew it was about you. I did not know how to look. My duties were taking me to a lumber camp in Russia. I met Zhao Tao there. He told me about you. The 'peculiar girl with the flower.' And here I am. I am not sure what I am supposed to do. You are his wife?"

"You are my husband's friend?"

"Yes."

"Then he will bring you to our home."

"He is not here?"

"No, he should be here tomorrow. He will come here by a truck along with some of the other village men."

"The train must be faster," commented Ju.

"Does he trust you?"

"Yes, he does."

"Ju, I know why you are here. You have been sent here to rescue my son. See him over there? He is playing. He is a girl. I have been hiding my daughter as a son. She has a hidden name, Hana, meaning 'one.' You were sent here to save her life. She will soon be discovered." Sun'hi's eyes pleaded with his.

He could feel himself racing down a pathway that was not of his choosing. However, had he ever made his own choices? *Yes,* he thought to himself. *I have chosen to love Sun'hi and to find her.*

"If my crime is discovered, her life will be taken or we will be sent back to Korea where we will surely die," she says, pleading with him. "Tomorrow when he brings you to our house, offer to take him, Zhao Yen, to the park and don't come back. You must love me by loving her enough to rescue her."

"What do I do then?"

"I don't know. But the same person who brought you here by just telling you to look, He will tell you what to do next. I just know you must leave this town."

"Who is that person?"

"He is the same one who gave us this love we have for one another, the love that I see in your eyes that is beyond understanding and would bring you so far to me and after so many years. I will say no more, as we are drawing attention by talking to each other. Ju, I was forced to be his bride. I love you and have never stopped."

CHAPTER SEVEN

THE RESCUE

"Hana, I want to tell you a story." Sun'hi is trying to help her daughter get ready for bed for the last time. She sits on the edge of her bed while Hana nestles under the covers. She is grateful for the opportunity to acquire a safe place for her Hana, but her heart breaks at the thought of never seeing her again. "You must be brave," she tells herself. Her love for her daughter is greater than her fear of pain.

"Mama, wake up. I think you fell asleep."

"I am sorry. Just deep in thought." She brushes her forehead to clear her mind. She must spend this limited time preparing her daughter for her escape. "Do you remember what happens to butterflies after they lay their eggs?"

"Yes, they fly very far away," answers Hana confidently.

"That's right. What happens to the eggs?"

"They are born and become caterpillars, and then they become beautiful butterflies."

"Like their mothers. Hana, you will become a beautiful butterfly somewhere far from here. I am going to send you with a friend tomorrow. He is kind. I can no longer hide you as a girl. Your father will soon discover who you really are."

Hana hugs her mother's neck. "Please do not send me away."

"Hana, I must protect you. Remember: I am always with you. I will always pray for you. And in this place of prayer, we will be together. Do you promise to be brave and become a beautiful butterfly?"

"I will be brave."

Deep inside, she knows Hana feels a sense of security. Sun'hi sings softly to her Hana and holds her all night long.

The next day, Ju meets Zhao Tao at the train depot. It has taken Zhao Tao a day longer to return to Fu Yuan. He gladly takes Ju to his home and to meet his son, Zhao Yen. Sun'hi barely looks at Ju when he enters their home. Ju hands Zhao Yen a present he has brought for him.

"May I take it, Father?" Zhao Yen asks.

"Yes, you may. This is my friend, Ju. I met him at the lumber camp. You may think of him as your uncle," Zhao Tao assures his son.

Zhao Yen unwraps the present. "A soccer ball!" he exclaims. "Thank you, Uncle Ju! May we go to the park and play, Father?"

"You may after dinner," answers Sun'hi.

"Please, Mom, may we go while you fix dinner?"

"It is okay. Sun'hi, I'll go get them when dinner is ready. It will give us a chance to spend some time together. I've been gone so long," Zhao Tao interjects.

"Okay, Zhao Yen, I'll help you get your shoes." Sun'hi gives in. While Sun'hi puts her shoes on, she speaks to her daughter for the last time. "Hana?"

"Yes, Mama?" Hana knows her mother is speaking to her about their secret when she calls her "Hana."

"This is the man I told you about last night. He is going to take you to the train. He has come to rescue you. You must be brave and not cry."

"I will be brave, Mama. He seems like a nice man."

"He is. Now give me a hug." Sun'hi holds her daughter close to her.

"Will I see you again, Mama?" Hana pleads.

"Let us both hope so." She gives Hana a final extra squeeze. She then exclaims loudly, "Run along, Zhao Yen! Be back soon for dinner!" She says these words almost as a proclamation of faith.

"I will. Uncle Ju will bring me to our home."

Sun'hi's heart leaps as Hana's words sound like a promise from the Father of Glory. She feels the dread leave her heart and hope replace it.

Sun'hi spends the time with her husband that he needs, which for the first time she is happy to do.

She fixes dinner slowly and suggests to her husband he go retrieve Zhao Yen and Ju. When he returns, he is in a panic. "They are not there, Sun'hi."

"What do you mean they are not there?"

"They are not at the park!" Zhao Tao speaks wildly.

"They must have taken a wrong turn. Did you ask around?" Sun'hi is trying to hold it together.

"Yes, but no one has seen them!" Zhao Tao says, choking back tears.

"You must go to the police!" encourages Sun'hi.

"I cannot. Zhao Yen is a ghost child. He doesn't exist. I was going to pay for a *hukou* after the ceremony," he explains, referring to the registration card.

"You don't think that stranger you brought home has taken him?" Sun'hi begins to cry. It is easy for her to cry because she has been holding it back ever since she hugged Hana at the door and waved good-bye to her for the last time. She is also feeling the loss of her child. She knows she isn't going to see her again, read to her, sing songs to her, or watch her grow up.

They both feel a growing sense of hopelessness, which lasts for the remainder of Zhao Tao's stay at home. Ju and Zhao Yen seem to have disappeared into thin air. They have become Ju and Hana. She appears to be his daughter, as she has more of the appearance of a Korean child than Chinese. No one is looking for a little girl.

Zhao Tao returns to Russia in a few days as planned.

***

Hana stays very close to Ju, closer than what Ju expected. The frightened child holds his hand as if she could hide inside it.

"Are you frightened, Hana?" He picks her up, and her small arms wrap around his neck. The conversation she had with her mother helps her to trust him. She isn't sure until she feels it in her own arms. "Shh, child, I will not leave you. I'll take care of you." He knows he will. Once on the train, they will travel all night long to Harbin. After a few minutes, Hana falls asleep. She is the first to wake up as the sun rays scatter about on the moving train. Hana talks about everything—the chairs they are sitting on, Ju's face, his clothes, her friends, what she sees passing by their window, but mostly she talks about her mother.

"So, you love your mother?"

"Oh, yes! She tells me stories—secret ones. I know when they are secret ones because she tells them to me in Korean. My dad knows some Korean. I talk to him mostly in Chinese. You know, he wouldn't like me if he knew I was girl. I was tired of being a boy. Now I can be a girl, just like my mom. I could beat all the boys at the park. None of them could run as fast as me, except for Sung-jin. He is older than me. If they knew I was a girl, they would have hung their heads in shame. Good thing I am a boy. I can jump higher than them too. One time, when we were playing football, I made a goal from the center line! Even Sung-Jin thought that was a great move. My dad is gone a lot. I only see him for a few days. He comes home to bring me candy. We have to be careful when he comes home not to speak Korean. He doesn't want me to speak Korean. He thinks Koreans are bums. He is not very kind to my mom. She is like his servant. She smiles much when he is not at home."

Ju nods his head and listens. He can't get over how many words a five-year-old could say. They take a little walk on the train and eat the lunch Sun'hi packed for their journey. They reach their destination when the sun begins to set. Exiting the train, Ju is uncertain where to go and whether he should ask for help. They begin to walk down the street as if he knows where he is going. By chance, out of the corner of his eye on a side street, he sees a building with a small cross on it. The beleaguered travelers walk toward the building, and Ju knocks on the door. He instantly feels fear. They are greeted silently by a young man who gestures to them to follow him without question though the building and out the back door.

They follow their silent guide down a narrow alleyway to the back door of a home. They are offered some food and given a place to rest. In the middle of the night, they are awakened by their guide, who takes them through a maze of alleyways with twists and turns that only a cat could possibly know. The guide finally leads them to an abandoned warehouse with many people inside who are worshipping God. The room is dimly lit yet filled with amazing light. They are both given new clothes. Ju feels an amazing love.

***

"Where are we?" Ju asks himself out loud.

"I think we might be in heaven," answers Hana. "Thousands of people are worshipping Jesus."

In reality, there were only about seventy-five individuals present in the room. "Mama and I worship Him by ourselves when no one is around. It is a secret like my name, Hana."

"Worship? What do you mean?"

"We would sing to the Father of Glory, just like these people are doing. But we worshipped him in Korean. I didn't think He knew Chinese. Now that was silly of me to think that, wasn't it? He knows everything." She listens more carefully. "Yep, that is Chinese. My father didn't worship. He does not believe. Do you, Uncle Ju?"

"Do I what?"

"Do you believe in Jesus?"

"I really don't know what you are talking about. I have never seen or heard anything like this before." He feels his heart being spoken to without words, which makes his mind incurably curious. From his backpack, he takes out the book he found in his parents' house and he pulls out the papers he inserted in the hidden pocket. He shows Hana a picture of a bearded man. "Is this who you are talking about?"

She examines it, and even though she is only five years old, she can read a few of the words in the caption. "Yes, this is Jesus, God's Son. He is the guy who removes our sin and gives us life. He died on this wooden thing called a cross. He stopped sin. He is the only pathway we need to heaven."

He feels lost in Hana's words. How could so many words come from a little girl? It is too much information for a brain that has never heard anything like that before. Suddenly, he feels very sleepy. A woman comes over to them and speaks to them in Korean.

"Do you speak Chinese?" she asks.

"I speak some, but my daughter speaks it very well." Saying the word *daughter* creates something invisible that will not let go. He feels he is in a partnership with Sun'hi. He will not leave Hana. He knows it. He feels he will give up everything for her.

"Sir, we will be leaving church soon, before dawn. We will take you to my home where you will be able to rest."

When the Chinese singing finally ends, along with the many words spoken beyond Ju's comprehension, before dawn and in the dark, they are led down a winding pathway though the back alleyways of the city to a home where they will be given a warm bed. Sleep comes quickly. How long Ju sleeps is unknown. The rest is much needed. When Ju wakes up, he is disoriented to say the least. Sun'hi, Hana, the train ride, the voices singing, the mazes—he is not certain what just happened. He feels lost yet strangely free. Is it really he who has chosen to go on this journey or has someone else chosen it for him? Is it Sun'hi? God? And what is God? "What did I think would happen when and if I found Sun'hi?" He speaks the last words out loud to himself. "I had to see her. I just want her."

Hana stirs next to him, still sleeping. He looks into her face. She captivates his attention. *How can someone so small take hold of your heart? I think she has made me rediscover my heart. I think my heart disappeared.* He feels his love for Sun'hi growing to a greater degree. Hana looks like her in her little-girl way. This little girl has pure trust in him. She doesn't question his care for her or that he will keep her safe. His thoughts turn suddenly toward Russia. "I have told my crew I will be back at eight in the morning in three days." He speaks to himself again. He realizes he is now on a journey that has no return and he has no knowledge of where he is going. "Who do I trust?" Again, he speaks out loud. "Russia. Russia. I have to return to Russia." *What about Zhao Tao? It has been a whole day since I left with his son.*

***

Meanwhile, Sun'hi and Zhao Tao have been waiting hours for Ju to return with Zhao Yen.

"Maybe they are lost?" Sun'hi hopefully suggests. "We could go to the park and look."

After their futile attempt to find their son, they return home.

"That Korean dog! I thought he was my friend. I am a fool!" he yells from deep within himself. All he feels is hatred. "I can't get help from the police because Zhao Yen doesn't exist. He has not been registered with the government yet. That dog has most likely sold him to make money. The dog. He has no soul."

"Russia!" says Sun'hi, hoping to sound helpful. She has been afraid to speak, afraid he will hear relief in her voice. This same man may have destroyed their *son* if he knew he was Hana. He would most likely have sent them back to Korea, which would mean death for them both. "Russia," she repeats. "Isn't he an official of some sort for North Korea's government? Doesn't he have to report to someone? Surely he will not jeopardize his high position?"

Zhao Tao turns to Sun'hi, and to her surprise, he replies, "You are right! He has to return to Russia. I will leave right away." Then it dawns on him again. "He has sold my son. I will destroy him somehow."

Sun'hi prepares a meal for him to take with him. She is thankful he will not be back for months. She wonders what will happen to her. It is a long moment for her. She has not thought of herself.

Ju will return for me. He came for me once, she reassures herself without any real hope. She quickly turns her thoughts away from herself to Hana. She comforts herself by thinking about where they have gone. *What are they doing?* "Hana, you mean 'one.'" She says it again, "Hana, you mean 'one.' Hana, you are my promise. *One.*"

CHAPTER EIGHT

AWAKEN, HANA

"Hana, wake up! Hana," Ju says. "The people who brought us here want us to have breakfast or lunch or dinner."

Hana wakes up slowly. She is crying. "Hana, what is the matter?"

"I want my mama." Ju picks her up and holds her. She wraps her arms around his neck. "I miss her. I want her to come with us. Please, can we go back and get her, Uncle Ju?"

Go back, he thinks. That is exactly what he wants to do, but they must go forward.

"Will you go get her?" Hana asks dreamily as she dozes back off to sleep.

"Hana," he says as he looks at the sleeping little girl. "Hana means one," he says to himself. He hears the promise in her name. "Hana." He realizes what has been in his heart all along. "I want to be with Sun'hi. I want her as my bride." He speaks to himself. "Yes, Hana, I want to get your mom," he whispers softly. "I want to get Sun'hi, your mother." In all the confusion in his mind, this was the one thing he knew for sure. *How? That doesn't matter.*

"Come down, sleepyheads!" an unfamiliar but friendly woman's voice calls for them.

"I am coming. Hana needs to sleep." Ju gets out of bed and finds his way into the hallway. It is a large home, and he feels lost. Finally, after a few wrong turns, he emerges into the kitchen where an older couple are sitting at the end of a large dining room table drinking a cup of tea.

"You have had a long journey. You must be hungry," says the lady of the house.

"Oh, yes, I am hungry," answers Ju.

"Come in here and sit."

The breakfast consists of egg rolls. The warm meal tastes good.

"Where is your little girl?"

"Oh, Hana is still sleeping. It was an exhausting journey for her."

"Where did you come from, Ju?" inquires the man, who happens to be a pastor.

"We just came from Fu Yuan. Hana was born there. She is my friend's daughter. I have been working in Russia as a wood inspector for the government of Korea and was sent on an official mission to choose the best grain of wood for a project for Kim Jong Eun. I am very trusted. I have never given them a reason not to trust me. I had no reason to leave—so I thought. However, there is something inside me that I did not know was there, and it is very strong."

"What would that be?" the lady of the house asks.

"I love Hana's mother. She was stolen from me the day we were to be married and sold as a bride by my own brother. I removed her from my heart and had to forget her. Then something strange happened to me. I was told to look for her. By chance, I met her husband in Russia and I befriended him. He invited me to his home. I went and found my bride living there with Hana. My Sun'hi was hiding her daughter from her husband by disguising her as a boy, naming her Zhao Yen. I found something else; I found my heart. I found love hidden there. I think she has been praying to something, and I am the answer to her prayer. My Chinese friend, her husband, was going to register Hana with the government soon. He would have discovered the truth. I was her miracle. I had very little time to act or think. I left with her daughter, headed southeast."

"How did you know where to go?" asks the pastor.

"I had been listening to an illegal radio in Korea before I came and had heard that there were people in China who help people and children escaping North Korea. I had heard their homes have a cross on them. I found one, and here I am. I had no intentions of leaving my country. But here I am," Ju relates his story.

"Did you say you were an official for your government?" the pastor asks.

"No, I was hired by the government to do official business. I know how to drive a truck. I had been to Russia already quite often, and I always returned. I wasn't planning to leave. I don't think I was, or was I?" Ju questions himself. "I just knew I was supposed to look, and I did pack my belongings and my life savings." He continues to try to understand himself. "I do not know what I was saving for. It seems nice to have my own money," Ju contemplates.

"Everyone who arrives at our door has gotten here by some sort of miracle," the lady of the house informs him.

"Do you know what you want to do next?" asks the pastor.

"I just know I can't go back. I want to get Sun'hi. I want her here with me."

"You say you can't go back, or is it you don't want to go back?" the man inquires, trying to get Ju to think. "Most people like yourself who have been dedicated to their country and are trusted to return have no reason to leave. They are able to go back." The pastor continues, "You must be dedicated to your dear leader, Kim Il Sung. Isn't he like a god to your people?"

"Yes, he is divine," answers Ju.

"What has changed?" the pastor challenges him.

"I am not sure. It started …" He paused, trying to understand himself. "I think it started when I fell in love with Sun'hi and …" He continues to contemplate. "When I returned to my parents' home right after Sun'hi was taken, I found this book." He took the book out of his backpack to show the man. "This book is about the life of Kim Il Sung. It explains his divinity. My parents wanted to join the party and were working hard to be accepted into it. They gave their lives for my brother and me for this hope. I found this hidden inside the cover." He pulls the hidden pamphlet from its carefully concealed place. It is obviously very old. "My mother's name is written inside it. My mother must have believed what is written inside it. When I found Sun'hi in China, I learned that she believes in God, whom she calls the Father of Glory. Somehow this could be the reason I was so drawn to her. She never told me this about herself …" He pauses for a moment before he continues, "Just like my mother. Finding this pamphlet has made me wonder …" He speaks slowly, as if he is afraid of what he is about to say. "… if this is hidden in my own heart from me."

"Let me see what you hold in your hand," the pastor gestures for him to hand it to him. He examines it, looking at the pages and the pictures inside. "Ah, this is a treasure. Look. It was printed in 1932." He flips through the few pages. "This tells the story of Jesus, His coming kingdom," he explains. "Do you know who He is?"

"No, sir, I do not. I don't know who I am anymore. I feel lost. I thought I knew who I was … Now? Now? Not only do I feel lost to myself, but I really don't know where I am going." Ju is becoming frustrated and is feeling threatened by his thoughts.

The pastor laughs. "This is a good place to be—to have lost yourself. This pamphlet is about the man Jesus, who is God's Son. His father is the Father of Glory you mentioned Sun'hi believes in. This Jesus once said, 'He who finds himself will lose himself but he who loses himself in me will find himself.' It sounds as if you have lost yourself." He laughs again. "You could lose yourself in Him, Jesus. Then you will find yourself."

"What do you mean?"

"Well, this Jesus is the creator. He became a man like us, and because He is the Son, He is able to lead us to His Father of Glory. This is the pathway you are on. He created you. He knows who you are," explains the pastor.

"Good thing somebody knows who I am. I feel as if I've been thrust out on a path that I did not decide to walk on. You know, I've been taught to hate people like you and what you teach. My government puts people like you in camps to die—not only you but your children and their children. I've seen them. They would put Sun'hi in a ..." His voice becomes quieter. "I would never see her again. They would want to destroy her. They would destroy Hana." He finishes quietly as if he is speaking only to himself. "This is what lies hidden in my heart."

"Ju ..." The pastor pauses. "Ju, do you want to lose yourself in Him?"

"Do I have a choice?" he continues. "It must be Him, the one whom you speak of who compels me on this unseen journey. He has sent me on it?"

"You do have a choice. You could make it back to Russia in time. You can leave Hana here, and we can take care of her. Sun'hi will continue to live her life—"

Ju looks up at him. "I don't want to go back ... I feel free ... freedom. I want to help Hana. I feel loved ... from way back ... into the now ... and ahead. I want to lose myself. I do. I want to lose myself in this mysterious unseen person you speak of. I believe what you are telling me. I think it may have already been there."

"Then just tell Him right now. Say His name 'Jesus,' and tell Him."

"Jesus, I want to lose myself in you. I want you to be the 'Son' for me who takes me to heaven. Forgive me. I can't be the *jusche* {the master of my destiny} and I want the same love that is in Sun'hi. to be in me. I want to go on this journey Sun'hi has prayed for. I want to keep Hana safe and rescue her." He pauses. "This is weird. Are You really there?" He walks across the room to a place where he feels he will not be heard and whispers, "Sir, please I ask for Sun'hi." Tears flow down his cheeks. He feels love flooding his soul. He senses himself. He senses Him, the one he just talked to for the first time. He whispers again, "I want to live in this place forever." The freedom he feels encircles him and swirls around him. He closes his eyes to let go. He opens them. "I am not alone."

"No, you are not. You are His. You have been made one with Him." The pastor turns to his wife. "This has been quite a breakfast."

"I would say. I think I saw heaven enter this room."

"I say we just enjoy the day. Tomorrow we will discuss practical plans," suggests the man. "Just to be sure, you want stay with Hana and help her? You do not want to go back to Russia?"

"I want to stay with Hana and take care of her," Ju answers confidently.

"Very well then. We will make plans in the morning."

"Plans for what?"

"Plans for your escape from China, of course."

"I can't stay here?" Ju is puzzled.

"No, you cannot stay. It would cause suspicion."

Ju remains silent.

"Do you still want to go on this unseen journey?" the pastor asks.

"Yes, I do, whatever it takes. I do not want to go back. I don't want to leave her. It would be like losing Sun'hi again." It felt good to Ju to make a choice that was his own.

As the men sipped on cups of tea the lady of the house has brought to them, they listen to the delightful laughter of the children. Hana has been asleep all this time.

The lady of house calls to Hana, "Awaken, Hana."

A little clear voice answers back, sounding very much like a chime, "Hana has awakened."

Hana finds her way to the kitchen much more easily than Ju did. She sees the welcoming plate of food and makes herself right at home. Her eager hands folded in her lap, she looks up at the lady of the house. "May I please eat?"

"Why, you certainly may. Hana is awake." She smiles at her little guest.

Hana giggles and begins to eat. She can hear other children playing. "Do you have kids?" inquires Hana.

"Yes, I do, and you may go meet them as soon as you are done eating."

It doesn't take Hana long, and she scrambles off her chair. "Where are they, ma'am?"

"Just in the next room."

Hana starts for the door.

"Hey, what about me?" a jilted Ju asks.

"Oh, Uncle Ju. I didn't mean to ignore you." She runs and gives him a hug. "Can I go play?"

"Yes, you may. Go quickly."

Before she leaves, she turns to the lady of the house. "I almost forgot. Thank you for the food."

"You are most welcome. Now, get going."

When Hana leaves the room, the lady addresses Ju, "Why, she is a bowl of sunshine, isn't she?"

***

The children are playing a chasing game and are running into each other. It doesn't take them long to acknowledge Hana.

"Hey, are you the new girl who came here the other morning?"

"I've been asleep that long?" Hana is shocked.

"Yeah, sleeping beauty," an impertinent boy speaks up.

"Ignore him." A girl about Hana's age comes to her defense. "My name is Sunja."

"And mine is Hana," Hana offers.

The group of about four children decide play a game of hide-and-go-seek. Hana hides with her newfound best friend Sunja.

"Where did you come from?" her new friend asks, once they are hidden from every one's view.

"The stars," answers Hana as her eyes look high above her as if she could reach the stars with them.

"Really? Which one?" inquires Sunja.

"The one that always shows up first in the sky, along with the moon."

"That is not a star; that is a planet," corrects Sunja.

"All right, I didn't come from a star." Hana sighs wistfully. "I came from Fu Yuan."

"Where? I never heard of that place. The name doesn't sound Korean," Sunja says indignantly.

"It's not; it's Chinese," Hana informs her.

"Chinese? Aren't you Korean?" she ask curiously.

"My mother is, and my father is Chinese. Where are you from?" Hana turns the tables.

"Korea."

"How did you come here?" Hana asks curiously.

"I crossed this river with my brother, and these people found us and they fed us. I was very hungry. I had not eaten in days. They brought us here. Now I eat every day. They tell us to believe in Jesus. We say we believe so they will feed us." Sunja gives Hana all the information.

"Jesus is my friend too. You sound like you have to believe in Him." Hana is perplexed. "That doesn't make sense to me," she continues. "I believe in Him because I want to. He protects me. He helped Uncle Ju and me to escape." Hana defends her friend Jesus.

"Escape what?" Sunja asks with interest.

"Not what but who—my father." She sighs and repeats, "My father."

"I don't have a father," Sunja offers matter-of-factly. "They will find us. No more talking," she warns.

"Too late, I found you." An annoying boy startles the two girls. "You two are as loud as two chattering squirrels."

"Listen, Pain," scolds Sunja, "I think you peeked, you cheater."

"I'm not a cheater," whines Pain.

"We will take our turn." She pauses and takes the opportunity to give him a shove. "Pain."

He takes off after her. But she is too fast for him and moves away from his grip. "Better go hide now, or you will have to be it again." She starts counting at lightning speed. And Pain takes off to hide along with about three other participants.

"Do you guys always have this much fun?" asks Hana.

Hana, Sunja, Pain, and the other children are immersed in play for most of the day, briefly stopping for a quick lunch and dinner. Feeling safe in this loving home they have found, they have adventures, going to places they will never go to or don't exist in this world, and the days seem to last ages. They have to be reminded a few times to quiet down by the lady of the house, but other than that, they play uninterrupted. Ju and the parents of the home enjoy watching them play and occasionally join in to help if a giant or some other villain or lost soul is needed. All in all, it is a good day for all.

"Time for bed, children. I'll be up to say a nighttime prayer with you!" calls the lady of the house, who must end the day.

"Here we go again," Sunja rolls her eyes.

"What?" wonders Hana.

"The prayer game."

"The prayer game? Silly, prayer is not a game."

"Can we keep you?" interrupts the lady of the house, who overhears the conversation. "Come, all you blessings. Let's get ready to play the prayer game. Who would like to go first?"

"I will," chimes in Hana.

"Go ahead, sweetheart," the lady says as Hana climbs into bed next to Sunja.

"Father of Glory, these guys think You are a game. They are silly, and we are having great fun. Maybe You will have to tickle them to show them how much fun You are. Thank you for taking care of me and my mom. Good night."

"You really do believe this Jesus is real?" whispers Sunja.

Hana just smiles and nods her head. "Your turn. Talk to Him for real."

"Jesus, Hana thinks You are real. Are You? I want to know. Maybe I could talk to You like Hana does. Good night." Each child follows Hana's lead and talks to Jesus for real, most likely for the first time.

The lady of the house gives each one a hug and a kiss before turning out the lights.

***

Morning comes early. Ju and Hana are invited to a morning family devotion to the Father of Glory. There is much singing and sharing about the Lord and reading the Bible. The pastor and his wife pray for everyone. And everyone prays for them. After they eat breakfast and clear away the dishes, the pastor asks Ju if he has a plan of escape.

"Escape?" Ju is perplexed. The idea is still new to him.

"Yes, what is your plan?" directs the pastor.

"Escape from what?"

"North Korea, of course." The pastor attempts to get Ju to start thinking.

"I already left there," answers Ju.

"You may have left there, but you have not escaped. Young man, you are still in China," the pastor continues. "If the authorities discover you, they will send you back," he explains further. "If you are involved in the black market or have official business, you are safe here in Harbin. Those two groups always return to North Korea." He pauses to observe Ju's reaction, and it is obvious this young man has no plan. "But you are a dissenter now that you have left your post. Well, maybe you have one good day left to be considered here on official business."

"Yes, I have until tomorrow morning before I report back. If the train is delayed to Russia because of the weather, I may have a little more leeway."

"The reason I ask is because you could wear your uniform for one more day and travel by train for two more days farther south."

"South?" questions Ju.

"Yes, south. You must leave China. I assume you had a fairly important job to be given enough trust to have a travel visa for Russia into China. Some people do hide in China for years. But I don't think you will be safe doing that. Besides, my guess is you have brought money with you that could help you out of China much faster than most." The pastor encourages Ju.

"Where would I go?" asks Ju timidly.

"I say, I've not met the likes of you before. You truly are out of step."

"You mean lost? Well, not anymore. I know where I am not going. I just don't know where I am going."

They both laugh. "This true of all of us. I will ask you point-blank. Do you want to go to America or South Korea?"

"South Korea?" He thinks about it. "Yes, South Korea. Why not?" Ju had not considered leaving his country. This is the first time it has occurred to him since he left and he does not have a plan. He had not planned to rescue Sun'hi's daughter. Now, she had become his daughter. He does not know he is now part of a network of individuals involved in helping people to leave North Korea.

"We help many people to leave North Korea," the pastor informs him.

"Many people?" he asks, surprised.

"Yes, there have been thousands who have left. Many never make it. They either die trying or are caught and sent back. Some we have to hide while we wait for money to be given to us to help them."

"Who are these people who give money to you?"

"People from South Korea, America, and other countries, not the countries themselves. Just individuals. They donate money to help people escape. Leaving doesn't come free," states the pastor.

"I did not know so many people are leaving."

"They are people who are unhappy. They want freedom. They are being persecuted for their beliefs. Mostly they are starving, and many are children. That is why so many children are here in our home." The pastor continues without interruption, "Others who live close to Tumen River patrol the area looking for children who have just crossed the river. They hand them over to others who bring them to this home. This is a safe house and one of many. No one knows each other so as to protect the network. You were brought here because you had a child with you." He pauses only for a moment. "Do you have money?"

"Yes," Ju answers with caution.

"I realize that is a personal question. But I need to know so we can figure out how fast we can get you out of here."

"I have all my money. Somewhere deep inside myself, I knew I wasn't going to return. But this is the first time I really thought about it."

"Your money can buy you a fast ticket out of here to Beijing. We want you to leave today." He pauses to allow Ju to absorb this information. "Now, you must listen carefully. I am going to take you to the train station. I am going to drop you off a few blocks away. You and your daughter will walk down the street until you see a house with a cross on the fence post. It is not very obvious. So keep your eyes open. When you get there, you will knock on the door and hand them this key from your right hand. Give it to the one who answers the door. Put it in her right hand. Later she will give you the key back. She will take you to the train station and buy your ticket for you. You will wait at a park bench. This may take a long time. Don't get nervous. Entertain your daughter, read, talk, and play. After you board the train bound to Beijing, get rid of your uniform. It will no longer be of any use to you. It could raise suspicion. Here in Harbin we often see people like yourself on official business. Often they are looking for refugees. I don't believe that is true in Beijing. They also may be looking for you. Be ready to leave in an hour."

CHAPTER NINE

THE CHOICE TO WALK ON THE FREEDOM ROAD

It all feels very unreal for Ju, as if he were watching a movie. He decides to put his regular clothes on underneath his uniform. The thought occurs to him he may have to ditch the uniform quickly.

As Hana leaves her newfound friends, there are hugs and tears. They make promises, like they will be best friends forever, and then there are more tears and hugs.

"We pray the angels go ahead of you and beside you and behind. May the Lord cover you and keep you safe," the lady of the house prays with her hands on their heads. She hands them a lunch she has prepared for their journey. The pastor then drives them a few blocks from the train station. They begin to walk slowly. Hana holds his hand, and that makes him feel stronger. She sings little songs along the way and picks up stray flowers or fallen leaves. She skips ahead and then runs back. After a while, he has to hold her hand firmly so he will not lose her, as the crowd is thickening. They finally find the house with the cross on it. A woman opens the door, and Ju places the key in her right hand from his right. He also hands her the needed money for the train ticket. She tells him to meet her at the train station. She will follow him from behind.

At the train station, all goes well. He sits on a nearby park bench, and she sits down next to them without acknowledging them. She leaves the tickets next to the park bench, along with the key.

"Always hand right to right. You leave in an hour. Board now." The nameless woman says all of this as she walks away.

Immediately, Ju takes Hana's hand and walks with the crowd to board the train heading for Beijing. Once he boards the train, he feels safe. It is a slower train, and it will take all night. Hana falls asleep in his arms. Ju soon falls asleep as well.

The morning sun grips his face and wakes him. The train makes a short stop, and new workers replace the old ones. They are checking papers. Hana befriends the lady next to him. He decides at that very moment to pay the woman a small fee to say the child is hers. She smiles and gladly takes his money. This time, they scrutinize his papers a little longer. It makes him feel uncomfortable. They question him about Hana, but the woman speaks up and states Hana is her granddaughter.

Hana overhears them speak. "He can't be the one. The report says he has a little boy with him, not a girl, and this man has no child."

When they are out of earshot, she tells Ju what the workers said. He realizes he has possibly been detected. The stop for Beijing is approaching so he takes his chance and enters the bathroom to rid himself of the uniform and official papers from North Korea. He replaces them with the fake papers that were given to him. He is now a South Korean traveling as a tourist with his son. The train comes to a stop while he is in the bathroom. When he gets back to his seat to retrieve Hana and thank the woman, Hana is not there and neither is the woman. Fear grips his heart. He looks out the window and detects the woman. She is dragging Hana away. He has a difficult time getting past the crowd and off the train. He loses sight of her but hears Hana call his name just before the woman turns the corner and heads down a street where she may have been lost forever. He catches up to the woman and grabs her arm hard, pulling her back. He takes Hana from her.

"Why are you doing taking my child?" he almost spits in the woman's face.

"You paid me to take her, you jerk. I was going to sell her, you idiot. I have a good mind to call the police and tell them you are a fake if you don't hand her over."

Hana jumps into Ju's safe arms and yells for all to hear in Chinese, "Daddy!"

They have to reboard the train with the fake papers.

Once on the train, Ju has a plan make Hana a boy again. When they are seated and concealed from the eyes of the other passengers he quickly takes off her long dress. Underneath, she is dressed in boys' clothes. He takes a baseball cap out of his backpack and places it on her head. He then puts one on his own. The caps bear the name of the Chinese basketball team, the Jinyu Ducks. She already has short hair. The North Korean official who has possibly been spotted with a little girl has disappeared.

The officials on the train are not concerned. There is a basketball game being played in Beijing the following day. They fit right in with everyone else who has come to view the game. As they draw nearer to their destination, time seems to stretch before them into the unknown. The fear lifts from his legs and arms, and he feels less shaky. He gets them under control. Hana sits beside him, showing him her basketball cards, chattering away in Chinese. Having lived most of her life as a boy, she easily falls back into the role. She really does have a love for the game. It was fostered by her birth father on the short visits he had had with her when he was at home. She is a great fan, as young as she is. After all, her life depended on it.

Ju feels an overwhelming sense of pride and love for her. As he enjoys her company, he can see Sun'hi in her. He then feels an overwhelming feeling of love and admiration for her. "Sun'hi," he says her name quietly to himself. "You are so beautiful to raise such an adorable child." Saying her name fills him with liquid love. He closes his eyes just to remember her and to feel her with him. His hand holds on to the brass handle beside him. The train gently sways him. It seems like only moments when it is time to exit the train.

When they exit the train, no one seems to notice them. They look like everyone else in the crowd. But they are not like everyone else. As they walk down the street, they are becoming overwhelmed with the immensity and wealth of the city. There are so many people and cars; everyone seems to own one. Ju wonders how they are ever going to find the help they need in a place like this. An individual notices Hana's cap and approaches Ju, offering to sell him tickets to the basketball game. The price is reasonable and within Ju's ability. Ju thinks it is unwise, frivolous, and foolish, but his daughter's pleading look melts his resistance. However, it is the right thing to do. What better thing to do for a little one who is enduring so much and being brave way beyond her years? It's an opportunity to give her a piece of her childhood. Ju feels he is breaking some unwritten law. "Don't ever enjoy yourself. Everything you do must be done for your country. Nothing can be done for selfish gain."

"Now, if that is true," Ju spoke to the unwritten rule, "why was I on a mission to help buy wood for a basketball court for the personal use of Kim Jong Eun?" His own thoughts shock him, and he looks around for someone who might betray him. "It's okay," he tells himself. "No one here cares. It is okay for us to go see the Beijing Jinyu Ducks play the Bay Rockets," he says as he reads the names off of the tickets. "We will take a break from this journey." He feels excited, having never watched a game before. He feels some unseen approval. Ju finds himself swept along with a stream of people heading to the arena. He starts to believe he just may be a real South Korean tourist. Just another droplet of water in this stream. As they approach the massive doors of the Olympic-size stadium. Someone takes their tickets. Luckily, the place is festive and friendly. Everyone belongs, and they have become part of the belonging.

One of the many attendants directs them to their seats; otherwise, they would have been lost. Ju and Hana are unprepared for what they see next. The stadium holds ninety-one thousand people. The seats are not all filled, but the crowd is loud and excited. Never have they ever seen anything like it. The basketball game is fast-paced, and they cheer for the Ducks. The game is close, and the team players get into a few tussles before it is over. What is surprising to Ju is seeing American players on the team along with the Chinese. Hana chatters away about the cheerleaders, the lights, and all the people. As quickly as it started, it is over. They walk out of the stadium bathed in light and color. The game has lasted until evening. The lights that show on the inside of the stadium glow through the walls.

"Look, Uncle Ju! The walls look like colors of falling water." She pauses only to shriek. "The green light is turning to pink!"

They have never seen so much light in the dark. Did they really live on the same planet as North Korea? One thing is for sure; Ju will never return even if he is physically taken back. He knows that everything he has ever been told about the outside world was a lie. Still dazed, they walk down the street and Ju signals for a taxi. As he speaks to the driver, Ju gives him a tip, which is really a bribe. "Take us to a home with a cross on it, please."

The taxi driver smiles and hands him back his tip. "You are with a brother. I know the way. And the ride is on me."

Ju feels strangely protected in such an alien world. The brother takes him straight to their destination. They salute him as he leaves. He walks up to the home with the cross and hands the lady who opens the door the key from his right hand to her right hand. They smile at each other, and they both know they are part of a secret kingdom, the kingdom of God.

Once inside, they are offered warm soup and bread. She doesn't speak much, as there is not much to say. Besides she only speaks Chinese. They stay there only a night before they are again taken to the train station. The woman brings them their tickets for a nonstop express train to Kunming. It is safer this way. Most refugees from North Korea cannot afford such a luxury and so the two can pass as tourists. Ju just needs to keep silent so his language will not betray him. Hana knows how to speak Chinese and does enough speaking for them both. They are both fortunate to have traveled so quickly in such a short amount of time because of his supply of money. It is possible they could be out of the country in a matter of weeks.

Once in Kunming, they have to follow the same procedure they had at the last two stops. The woman hands Ju the key before they part. Kunming is vastly different from Beijing. It is much smaller and warmer. Palm trees sway in the breezes, and the people are far more diverse. Faces emerge from various cultures and ethnicities. Not everyone here is Chinese or even Asian for that manner. They speak various languages. Ju and Hana stroll down the street before calling for a taxi. They walk around the neighborhood, and on their own, they happen to find a home with a cross on it. They knock on the door and hand the young teenage boy the key. He takes it without question. He lets them inside. They are offered a warm supper and told they are in luck because tonight is their church service.

At about 2:00 a.m. in the morning, people start to arrive at the home. The house is packed with about fifty men, women, and children. Hana sits on Ju's lap, as she does not want to lose him. When the congregation sings, they sing very softly. Then a pastor stands up and begins to speak about love. The greatest love, he says, is to give up all you have for someone else. That is a selfless love. This kind of love is the greatest love people have for people. What Jesus did for us was the greatest. He gave up heaven and then His very life to remove our sinful nature by taking our place on the cross. He died for the whole human race. The Father has such great love for us that He gave up His own Son for the good of all.

Ju does not understand what is being said. Hana is trying to translate the message for him. However, he feels as if he is experiencing this love. He realizes how much Sun'hi loves Hana to give her up and to trust him. How did she know she could? Maybe it isn't him she trusts but God Himself.

I am glad she did, because now I am loved and I believe I am giving this same kind of love. I've given up everything, but really I gave up nothing. I have Hana now.

The people at the meeting want to pray for their safety. They surround Ju and Hana as they pray for angels to protect them and the blood of Jesus to cover them. They pray they will have courage and strength and health. One person prays they will be made invisible. When all is said and sung, the group leaves the home by small groups. Most of people give them hugs and words of encouragement.

CHAPTER TEN

THE DOCTOR
AND HIS WIFE

One couple informs them they will be coming with them. Ju grabs their belongings and follows along with Hana into the night. The couple owns a car. It is just before, dawn, and they drive for a long way. They are instructed to hide under a seat that is easily removed and then covered by a tarp. It is a small area, and they are cramped. But they manage it. Ju accidently leaves the backpack on the seat. There is a checkpoint they have to go through when leaving Kunming. The couple tells them they are headed to a town very close to Laos by the name of Jinghong. At the checkpoint, the inspector questions the couple.

"Doctor, what is the backpack you have on the seat? I am going to have to inspect that."

He reaches for it and is about to open it when the doctor interjects, "Sir, I must warn you that bag contains medical waste that needs to be properly disposed of. You should not touch it." The doctor speaks calmly but with firmness.

The checkpoint guard almost drops the bag before throwing it back into the car. "You may pass through," the guard releases the doctor, and they let him through without further inspection. The travelers drive for another hour before reaching the couple's home. It is then they are allowed to get out. The woman is angry with Ju but says nothing. She just glares at him, which is far worse than any words she could have spoken. Ju feels shame for making such a terrible mistake.

"I am most sorry," he tells the doctor once she leaves the room. He is too afraid to speak while she is there.

"All is forgiven, young man. She is afraid to have you here. It makes her nervous," he consoles Ju. "We help people like yourself a few times a year to keep our operation here a total secret." He continues to explain, "We have been most successful because we are so careful. She is truly happy to have you here. It is the passion of her heart to help grant you your freedom." He pauses for a moment. "This is the last stopping place before you leave China. You will live with us for a short time."

At this point, the woman reenters the room. "I do forgive you, young man," she says sternly. She continues with no smile. "You must absolutely understand everything we require you to do must be followed perfectly. You cannot jeopardize this safe house again." She makes eye contact, and Ju cannot pull his gaze away. "Not only do you jeopardize yourself but all those who can be helped in the future. We are highly respected in this community, which helps to protect you." She pauses to make sure she has his complete attention. "No one can know you are here. You cannot go outside. You have been given a room in the inner part of the house. It has no windows. There is a connecting bathroom. Under no circumstances are you to leave this area. I will bring you your meals. I'll try to find more books or games to help entertain the child." A glimmer of compassion starts to appear in her voice. "Do you have a Bible?"

"No, ma'am, I've never touched one. I've seen others hold one in their hands while they read from it," answers Ju.

Hana speaks no words; she just holds on to Ju's neck very tightly.

"I will find you one. It will give you something to read while you wait to leave China. You can learn about the Father of Glory," she suggests, "learn about what He thinks." She insists abruptly, "Turn the child around."

Ju almost has to pry Hana's arms off of his neck.

"It's okay, Hana," he consoles her.

The woman's voice softens. "I just need to speak to you, child. What is your name?"

Ju begins to speak. "Han—"

"I didn't ask you. Now did I?"

Ju is immediately silent.

"Tell me your name, daughter. It's okay; I am really not mean, just stern."

"Hana," she answers in a whisper.

"Speak up, young lady."

"Hana," she repeats more clearly.

"You are not a boy?" the woman keenly asks.

Hana looks up to Ju for direction.

"It's all right." He nods in approval.

"No, madam, I am not a boy."

"You play the part of a boy very well. But why?" she inquires.

"At first, my mom had to hide me as a boy or my real father would have killed me."

The woman looks into Ju's face with stern admiration. "You are escaping from North Korea with a child that is not your own?"

"Yes, madam," he confesses.

"Yet she has become your own."

"Yes, madam," he agrees.

"She looks at him for a long moment without saying a word, as if she can read his story by studying his face. Her focus returns to the child. "Hana," she says sternly. "Hana, look at me."

Hana looks the woman in the eye.

"Under no circumstance are you to leave these rooms. It will not be easy, but you must obey."

"Yes, madam, I will not leave these rooms." She receives the woman's instruction.

The doctor then speaks. "Thank you, dear, for your help." He puts his reassuring hands on her shoulders. He directs his attention to Ju and Hana. "You will be here for a week or two; the border, for whatever reason, has tightened their measures for those crossing the border." He continues, "You will stay here until the situation changes and they loosen their hold." He smiles warmly. "During your stay, we hope to make you as healthy as possible for your journey through Laos. When you leave our home, a guide will help get you across the border. This guide has certain expenses." He pauses. "Do you have any money of your own?"

"Yes, sir, I do." Ju continues, "When I lived in North Korea, I was a wood inspector and was sent to Russia's lumber camps on numerous occasions, and I made money on the side, which I saved. I brought all of it with me." He sighs. "At the time, I had no plans of leaving. I just had a slim hope of finding …" and then he stops. "Finding Sun'hi." Ju is caught in a wave of deep love when he says her name. *How does she do this me?* he wonders. He doesn't want to let go of the moment. "Sun'hi is Hana's mother. She was praying to Jesus for help. And He sent me. I really don't know who He is; I just met Him in the past weeks, although He has known me all along."

"You will do fine here, and you are safe and in good hands." The doctor nods to his wife. "I'll take you to your room."

In the large room, Ju sees a few beds, a table, and some chairs. There are books and games on a shelf.

"Make yourself comfortable. There is a calendar to help keep track of the days and a daily schedule hanging on the wall. We have found other individuals who have stayed here do much better if they regulate their time. It helps keep them from becoming stir crazy. Make yourself comfortable," says the woman.

"My wife will bring you breakfast shortly. My name is Doctor Sung Jin, and my wife's name is Ze Annchi."

She nods her head. "Afterward you may rest. Here is the Bible I promised you," Ze Annchi hands him the book.

"I can't read Chinese." His eyes look downward.

"It is written in Korean." She grins.

"Korean?"

"Yes, it was printed in South Korea. There are many Christians who live there. And they do not have to worship in secret like we do here. They are freer than we are here."

Ju thought, *I've been gone for such a short time. How different I feel and think.*

The next morning, they are awakened by a command from Ze Annchi. They are given another breakfast. Afterward, they begin a new exercise program right inside the room, which they repeat again later in the day. They begin reading the Bible. Ju reads the Bible for the first time to Hana. They start in the book of Genesis and also the book of Luke. Hana suggests they act out the stories. It is Ju who has the idea to teach Hana how to read and how to add and subtract. So they begin their school.

Ze Annchi comes in later and offers to read to Hana from some picture books. She has the ability to make the stories come alive. Hana snuggles up to her while she reads. After she leaves, they continue the school lessons until dinner.

Jin and Ze Annchi join them for dinner and offer to teach them how to play Chinese checkers. On nights when they do not join them, Hana and Ju play by themselves, hoping to develop some skills for the game so they could possibly beat the couple. The time goes by quickly, and they are able to handle their confined living quarters quite well. The whole group are risking their lives for freedom.

One evening, while Ju is tucking Hana into bed, she looks up at Ju and asks him, "Did you know my mom before you came to our house?"

"Why do you ask such a silly question?" he wonders.

"Well, I saw something in my mom's eyes and yours when you first came to our town." She pauses as thinks about what to say next. "I can see you are friends and not strangers. And you are not her brother either," she challenges.

Hana doesn't wait for Ju to answer. He is left speechless. "Did you know her in North Korea?"

"Yes," answers Ju. This child's insight amazes him.

After a moment, Hana thinks about Ju's answer before asking the next question. Her face lights up like she has just solved a mystery. "You love my mom, like a boyfriend loves a girlfriend?"

Ju smiles. "Yes, Hana, I do," and then he becomes sad. "She was going to be my bride."

"What happened? Did you get in a fight?" she wonders.

"No, she was stolen from her country and from me and sold to your father."

"You came to our home looking for my mom?" She smiles at her own insight. "You love me because you love my mom." She knows she speaks the truth.

"This was true at first, but now it is also true that I just love you. I love you as a father loves his daughter." He gives her a fatherly hug.

She gives him a daughterly hug. "I like it that you love my mom. You must love her a lot." Suddenly, Hana is quiet. She is thinking about Ju and her Mom and then only her mom. "Daddy?" She speaks the term of endearment for the first time ever. "I miss my mom. I miss my mom real bad." She begins to cry. She cries for a very long time while her daddy holds and rocks her.

CHAPTER ELEVEN

THE STORY DAYS

One morning after the day's school is finished, Hana wants Ju to read to her the story about Isaac's servant, who was sent to get Rebecca for his wife. Hana suggests, "Let's act this story out. I'll be Rebecca, and you be everybody else. I am at the well, but first you have to pray."

Ju recites what Hana dictates to him. "Lord, God of Abraham, please show me who is the right bride for Isaac for I cannot take Isaac with me. Let it be the young lady who when I ask her to let down her jar of water into the well to give me a drink says 'yes,' and she will also say, 'Let me draw water for all your camels also.' Let her be the one."

Ju pretends to walk a long way as Hana begins to narrate.

"The servant of Abraham walks a long, long, long, very long way with his camels through the hot desert. He has to fight sand storms …"

Ju makes a howling noise and hides his face.

"Bandits!"

Ju fights with a pretend sword in the air.

"Climbs mountains!"

He climbs over the beds.

"Finally he is there at the well of Abraham's relative. A beautiful girl is there, and he asks for water."

"Young lady, will you draw water for me?" says the servant/Ju.

"Yes," begins Rebecca/Hana. "And I will also draw water for your camels."

"This is the one," whispers the servant. "Take me to your parents. You have some, don't you?"

"Yes, Nahor is my dad, and Mihah is my mom," says Rebecca.

The servant and Rebecca go off together.

"Daddy, you forgot to ask my name?" Hana whispers.

"Oh, yes," he whispers back. And with a louder volume, he says, "What is your name?"

"Rebecca," answers Rebecca. "Here we are. This is my home. Mom, Dad, come! There is a man here to see you." Rebecca turns to face the servant. She is now pretending to be the mom and dad.

"Yes, what do you want?" Hana lowers her voice deeply like a man's.

"I would like to take your daughter to my servant Abraham to be a bride to his son Isaac. Do you remember Abraham?" states the servant.

"Yes," Rebecca's father Nahor says. Hana continues in her deep voice, "He was a cute little kid, and now he is all grown up with a child?"

"Well, yes, his name is Isaac and he is not a child but a grown man."

"Oh, we will ask Rebecca what she wants to do," says Nahor.

Rebecca now answers, "I will go with him. Just let me pack my bags."

"Here is your money for your daughter," says the servant.

"So, off they go," narrates Hana. "They climb mountains."

Ju and Hana climb over beds.

"They fight with bandits."

They both fight with swords.

"And they walk a very long, long, long, long way. When they get there, Rebecca says, 'Is that him?'"

"Yes, it is," says the servant.

Ju then switches to being Isaac, and Hana runs to him and jumps into his arms.

"I am your bride."

"And now you will be my wife."

"The end!" says Hana.

"Again, again, Daddy. Let's play it again."

After numerous times, Ju pauses. "I believe God is speaking to me, Hana."

"What is He saying?" she inquires curiously.

"He is telling me I am like Isaac, and when we get to South Korea, I must send a *servant* to where your mother is who was my bride, and I'll give money for her and buy her back. The servant will bring my bride to me so she can be my wife."

Hana hugs Ju. "I'll have my mother back," she says hopefully.

"Yes, you will have your mother back," reflects Ju.

They are interrupted by Ze Annchi.

"You thespians, it is time for dinner!"

"Already?" Ju exclaims.

"Yes, already."

Ju's heart fills with such joy, expectation, and purpose. He whispers to Sun'hi, "I am coming for you, Sun'hi. You will be mine again."

The following day, Hana suggests, "Let's play when Isaac is going to be sacrificed."

"Okay, Hana, we haven't played this one in a little while." He rolls his eyes.

"You be Abraham, and I'll be Isaac," directs Hana.

"Yes, madam!" He salutes her, and she laughs.

"Oh, Daddy!"

Ju starts without further instruction. "You go first, Hana."

Hana pretends to be God, and in a low voice, she says, "Abraham, take your son, your only son, to sacrifice him."

"Yes," answers Abraham/Ju, and he addresses his son, Isaac, played by Hana. "Come, Isaac. We are going on a trip up the mountain for the sacrifice."

"I am ready, Dad. Do you want me to gather sticks?" She pretends to gather sticks. "Dad, where is the sacrifice?"

87

"The Lord will provide," answers Abraham.

"Well, this is an easy trip up the mountain since we are not dragging along a ram."

"As they go, they sing a song," directs Hana.

They hum a little tune.

"Finally they are at the top."

They climb on top of the bed.

"Come, Son." Abraham picks Hana up and lays her down on the pretend altar. He raises a pretend knife.

"No, Abraham, stop! Stop!" God yells. Hana says in a deep voice, "I'll provide the sacrifice. Look! There is a ram."

"Isaac jumps off the altar and places the ram on it."

"Bravo! Bravo! Very good!" Ze Annchi has been watching from the doorway. "Did you know that story is a picture of God the Father giving His Son to us? That is why God says to Abraham, 'I will provide the sacrifice.' And when Isaac jumps off the altar, that is a picture of His resurrection. Dad and Son are joined together again," Ze Annchi explains.

"Along with a bunch of new brothers and sisters." Ze Annchi smiles. "You two are such great fun. I am going to miss you when you leave. I have to finish your supper. I'll be back a little later. Maybe I could read you a story."

Hana is thinking deeply about what Ze Annchi said about the picture. "You know, that is like my mom. She had to let go to save me, and we will be reunited again, like God and His Son." She continues her thought, "God sent His Son here in this world to save all of us, to bring all of us to Him." After pausing to think again, she says, "My mom really loved me to let me go. I know she was sad about it. But she said I must be brave, and I told her I would be brave. But I am not alone. Ju is with me. I will see her again."

Ze Annchi picks her up and holds her.

"You will, lioness. Your faith is like a roaring lion in the earth. And your name, *Hana*, speaks. Your mother named you well. One, I have to fix us dinner. Maybe tonight I could read you a bedtime story." She sets Hana down on the ground.

After dinner, Ze Annchi comes to Ju and Hana's room. Hana runs to her and takes her hand, inviting her into the room.

"You came to read to me after all, Ze."

"Dear, I always keep my promises. But this is not a story from a book. It is one my mother used to tell me when I was a little girl."

"You were a little girl?" Hana is surprised.

"Yes, silly. We are not born old. I used to play and have fun like you. Do you want to hear the story?" Ze Annchi rolls her eyes.

"I do want to hear the story. I am ready." Hana giggles.

"Come sit next to me."

Hana climbs into the chair, and Ze sits down beside her and puts her arm around her. "Is that better?"

"Much better," says Hana.

"Once there was a man who took care of sheep," begins Ze Annchi.

"Is this a Bible story?" Hana inquires.

"No, but it does teach us a lesson. This man had some trouble one night. He found out that some of his sheep were missing. When he walked around the fence that held the sheep, he found wolf tracks and a hole in the fence."

"Did the wolf eat some lambs?" Hana worries.

"I don't know if he did or not. But I guess he could have. Well, his neighbor told him, 'You should fix the hole in the fence.' But the man replied, 'The damage is already done. The sheep are gone. There is nothing I can do to make a difference.' The next day, when the sheep herder awoke, he found to his dismay more sheep were missing from the fold. When he checked the hole near the fence, sure enough, there were fresh tracks from the wolf. This time, the owner listened to his neighbor's advice and repaired the hole in the fence. This stopped the problem."

"What is … Can I call you 'Grandma'?" Hana asks, looking up into Ze's eyes.

"You most certainly can, dear. It would warm my heart," Ze held her closer.

"What is the lesson of the story, Grandma?"

"Often, bad things may happen to us. They do happen. We can only learn from our mistakes. Don't ignore your mistakes. Learn from them, and fix the problem. This way, you will avoid future losses."

"I like that story. Can you tell another, Grandma?" she begs, not wanting her to leave just yet.

"I suppose I can. This one is a funny story."

"Oh, I like funny stories."

"I do too. Once there was a strange animal brought to a village by some merchants. Everyone was excited about it, and people came from far away to see it. It was extremely large but gentle in nature. There happened to be four blind men who came to see the animal—"

"How can blind men see? Blind men can't see," reasons Hana.

"No, you are right; they cannot see with their eyes, but they do see with their hands."

"Oh, I see," Hana teases.

"Said the blind man," says Ju, who has been resting and taking the whole thing in.

They all laugh.

Ze continues her story, "The first blind man held the animal's nose. 'This animal must be a radish. It is very long and bends.' The second blind man held the animal's leg. 'You, sir, are wrong; this animal is like a column. It is straight and tall.' The third blind man feels the animal's side. 'You are both wrong; it must be a wall. It is hard and long and straight.' The fourth blind man held the animal's tail. 'This animal is like a rope; none of you can possibly be right.' The four men argue for a whole week. Not one would give in to the other. Do you know what kind of animal it is, Hana?"

"Well, let me see … It was large and …"

"Gentle," adds Grandma.

"Flexible like a radish, tall like a column, it is like a wall, and it has a tail like a rope. What color is it?"

"Gray."

"Is it an elephant?" she guesses.

"Yes, it is. You are very smart. Will you be smart enough to know in the midst of a problem or situation that sometimes we are too close to it to get the whole picture? We have to step back and listen to what others have to say. This helps us to come to a better conclusion."

"I like this story too. The blind men were funny."

"I think it is time for my bedtime. I must be going," says Ze Annchi.

"Oh, I don't want you to leave," whines Hana.

"I think it is bedtime for you too, Hana," interjects Ju. "Give Ze a kiss good night."

"Grandma! Grandma, a kiss good night." Hana gives Ze a kiss good night. And "Grandma" gives a kiss in return.

"God bless you. And may He give you good dreams."

"You too."

"Good night, Ju."

"Thanks, Grandma." Ju smiles in appreciation.

"May you, Ju, remember the lessons these stories teach in the days ahead." Ze closes the door.

CHAPTER TWELVE

FOREVER WAS GONE, AND THE AMERICAN ARRIVES

Dr. Sung Jin comes to Ju and tells him it will be another two weeks before it is safe to leave. The border patrols are securing the borders. Some refugees have been caught and sent back. The announcement makes them feel like they will stay in their home forever. Maybe that isn't so bad. They are feeling quite comfortable and safe. Outside the house's walls is uncertainty. Suddenly, just as forever came, it is gone.

The doctor comes a few days later, wakes them in the predawn hours, and tells them to get ready. Their guide will meet them outside where they will get into a taxi. They will travel closer to the border crossing where many tourists cross to go on day river trips on the rivers in Laos. When they get there, they are not to act like they recognize him, only follow his lead. He acts like a tour guide for tourists. His cover must not be compromised. It is true he helps tourists from China and other countries to plan these trips. However, he is also able to sneak in some escaping refugees.

Ju and Hana get ready quickly. They pack their meager belongings while the doctor continues to instruct them. "You will go out our back door and through the backyard gate. Turn left in the alley, and in about four hundred steps, turn right into another alley. Take another seven hundred steps, and turn left on the street. The man will be waiting for you. Hand him the key so he knows he has the right person. The neighbors are sleeping so they will not know you have come from our home. Just so you know, he is an American."

"American?" responds Ju with distrust.

"Yes, he is Korean American. He has many connections and knows how to help North Koreans across the border."

Ju's and Hana's things are packed. Ze Annchi hands them a backpack full of food and medicine for the journey. There are tears in her eyes. Hana runs up to her and hugs her tightly.

"I will miss you, and I will always remember you." She pauses. "I love you, Grandma."

"I will miss you too, my little one, as if you were my own. And I will pray for you *every day*."

"Thank you," says Ju, shaking Dr. Sung Jin's hand. "Thank you. Thank you. Thank you."

"Go quickly." The doctor urges them to go, not wanting to express his feelings, in case he is unable to control them. "Go quickly. You have been like a faithful son." He lowers his eyes.

They walk down the stairs in the home they have stayed in for about a month. They walk outside into complete darkness. The air is cold, and their lungs feel painful as they gasp their first breaths of fresh air in weeks. They approach the back gate, and Ju silently picks Hana up in his arms. They make no sounds, and the shadows of the alley help to conceal their fear. They are doing as they have been instructed without looking back. When they reach the street, they find a car is waiting for them. Ju hands the stranger the key, and he motions for them to sit in the backseat. Without turning around and speaking to them in what sounds like Korean, the stranger says, "What took you so long?" He speaks sharply. "I almost had to leave you."

Ju feels like defending himself. It is enough that he is with an American.

"My apologies, sir." He swallows his pride, and it goes down hard. Hana hugs Ju more tightly.

"Now, listen carefully. When we reach the hotel that you will stay in close to the border area, I will walk ahead of you. It is a long walk to the hotel, as they do not park close."

The American wears a long coat and dark sunglasses. It is hard to keep up with him. He walks fast but appears to walk slowly and acts like he is the only person on the planet. He is taller than most. This helps Ju not to lose sight of him. Ju has not walked in the open in weeks. His legs feel heavy and stiff. The sun is starting to rise, and it is painful to his eyes. But he forces himself to watch his guide. He enters the hotel they are to stay in before boarding the bus the following day. They wait a few minutes before they enter and hand the receptionist their prearranged reservations. For all intents and appearances, they look like South Korean tourists heading to Laos for a day river trip on the Nam Ou. The clerk hands them their keys and shows them to their rooms. Much to their surprise, there are three other people in the room, an older man and a young couple. They enter the room in silence and without questions.

Later that evening, the American they had followed comes to the room. He smiles at them and encourages them. "You did well. You have met your new neighbors?"

The five of them had not really spoken, as the uncertainty had warned them not to share much information with each other, not even names. The American introduces them to each other.

"These will be your traveling partners through Laos to Thailand. You will not be leaving right away but soon. You will be traveling as a group of South Korean tourists. Now remain in your rooms until I return. Do not leave. I will be back in a few days." He leaves them with a small bag of groceries.

A few days go by with no sign of his return. The group starts to discuss the idea that one of them should leave and look for him.

"No!" says Ju with a commanding voice. He is beginning to weaken. He is feeling angry at this American, whom he feels has abandoned them. The food is getting low and will run out soon.

It is eight days before their guide returns. It has not been easy. He enters the room and smiles. The group does not express their anger, as they are greatly relieved to see him.

"Oh, good. You have not torn each other apart. I had trouble getting your passports. They wanted more money for a payoff. We must leave tomorrow, as that is the day the passports are good for. No more waiting." He places his hand on Ju's shoulder and compliments him. "Thank you for holding the group together and not letting anyone leave."

"How did you know?" Ju is amazed.

"I just guessed. You just seem like a leader to me." He continues to address the whole group, "We will board a bus, which will take us to the checkpoint about twenty miles away. The checkpoint is about two miles from the stop, and we will walk to it. It will be the beginning of a very long walk for you …"

Hana finds her voice and asks a question she can no longer keep to herself.

"Are Americans Korean?" she inquires.

The American looks down at her and laughs. "No, little one, Americans are from every country in the world. White Americans would be noticed right away here in China. I look more the part. Sometimes I am Chinese here and not American."

The warmth in his smile makes everyone relax.

"Listen, I know you are all frightened. When we reach the border, my friend and I will speak English. I understand, Ju, you speak a little Chinese. Only answer questions with yes and no."

***

The next morning, they leave as a group to board the bus. Ju and Hana board the bus with no problems. Hana has so many questions but instinctively remains silent. They look out the window with great interest. The terrain is different from what they are accustomed to. Palm trees border the road, and it is fairly flat. There are a few people talking about the day's adventure. The bus makes numerous stops. People seem to know each other. The stops become less frequent as they begin to travel outside the city. Finally the bus stops and their guide exits the bus along with some other day travelers. Ju and Hana and the other three get off with other travelers. Appearances must be kept up.

"Once you cross, you will travel on the river, but then you must exit and travel east where you will meet with a travel guide who will direct you to Thailand. There are guides who look for refugees like yourself. They will want payment for their help and will lead you to the South Korean Embassy in Thailand. Once you cross the border, you should be safe from man. The natural elements will prove to be challenging. The terrain is rough through the mountains. Don't despair, and use common sense." The American gives his last instructions.

At the fairly remote checkpoint, they are asked questions and searched. The American pays the guards a bribe to move the group through quickly. They are allowed through without much trouble. But just as the last one crosses the border, they hear sirens. The American yells at them to run quickly into the woods. They do as they are told. They can see from the cover of the woods that the American who led them is being questioned. They are close enough to hear. Hana understands everything and is able to translate.

"They are calling him a liar. They believe he has been helping North Koreans to cross the border into Laos. He tells them they are wrong. He is telling them, 'I am an American working for a travel agent for Chinese and South Korean tourists,'" Hana relates to the group.

They slap him and begin searching him. The refugees are horrified as they watch him being arrested. The police are yelling at the border guards, demanding to know how many have crossed the border into Laos today. They lie to the border patrol; they are afraid of being reprimanded. They do not give them an answer.

"He, the American, is the only one who has tried to cross today other than those standing in line. We stopped him." They try to protect themselves. "Maybe the group he was trying to help is still coming." Sure enough, another group much like theirs is seen walking toward the checkpoint. They become aware of the approaching danger too late. They pretend not to recognize the American. They too are arrested and carried away.

"We just made it, Hana," Ju holds her closer.

"Will they kill the American?" she asks.

The group continues to stare in disbelief. They hide in the woods for what seems like a long time, not wanting to be seen. After they feel safe, they move away from the border. Having lost their guide, they are uncertain as to what their next move should be. The girl and the boy break into a dead run.

Ju yells, "Stop running! Stop running!"

They listen to him and stop as if they too have been caught.

"They can't get us. Come back!" he yells. "You are running in the wrong direction. We need to do as the American told us. We are to continue to act like day tourists and rent the boats at the river. The river will take us south. Instead of returning, we will continue to head east until we reach a foot trail."

The men and the woman who are in the group look at him but do not answer.

"Listen, I know what we saw back there was terrifying. But right now we are safe and our worst enemy is ourselves. Please, let's stick together as a group. Look. There are signs directing us toward the boat launch."

"What do they say?" asks the younger man.

"They are telling us to follow the pathway for about half a mile and we will find the boat launch," answers the older man.

"You can read Chinese?" asks Ju in amazement.

"Yes, I have been hiding in China now for about five years, working in various restaurants or other situations. I have learned some during my stay."

"I, for one, am not moving another step until we know each other's names," blurts out the young woman. "My name is Kang." She nudges her younger companion. "This is my younger brother."

He doesn't respond.

"Tell them your name."

"Chang," he answers reluctantly.

"My name is Hana," answers Hana without further prompting.

"Thank you, Hana. You are cute and brave."

"I don't mind if you know my name. Is there a reason why we shouldn't? Everyone seems afraid," says Hana.

"We were told not to share our names just in case we were caught. We would not have information that might have hurt others in our group," explains Ju. "But I am pretty sure we are somewhat safe now. We can at least share our names. Mine is Ju."

They all turn to the older gentleman.

He answers with a smile, "Mine is Shin." Shin takes the lead on the pathway to the boat launch and approaches the waiting attendant. He asks him what the fee is in Chinese.

The attendant answers in broken Chinese. "There is an extra fee for those who do not return and one for our silence."

Shin shares the added information. He smiles and gives them the required fee and the demanded bribe. After being paid, the attendant gives them some advice. "Take the boat to the farthest drop-off point. There is a cabin nearby for those who take *overnight* trips. You are welcome to use it for one night only. Leave the boat, and follow the footpath east. If you take the boat beyond this point, we can have you arrested for stealing."

It is late afternoon as they continue their journey. The sun is shining and seems to promise them a clear evening. The boat has a small outboard motor for returning upstream. They decide to use it to speed down the river stream. For a time, the group enjoys the thought that they are day tourists from South

Korea. The sun warms their hearts and puts smiles back on their faces. It is a good hiding place for their fearful thoughts. Their faces wear the delusion well. And for a time, they fool their own minds. It is about sunset when they reach what they believe is the last drop-off point. They have passed several on the way, observing real tourists leaving their boats and taking dinner breaks at quaint cafés before returning to their boats. The last drop-off point has several cabins to stay the night in, and a few are already occupied. As they dock the boat and tie it to the pole, Shin warns, "I don't believe we should stay here."

"I agree with you," says Ju. "It doesn't feel safe."

"The attendant was easily paid off, and it would not hurt him in the least to be paid for telling an official our whereabouts."

"You are right; he cannot be trusted." The girls sigh at the thought of giving up a shelter for the night.

"We will start heading east. It will be twilight for another hour. Maybe we will find a foot trail."

Darkness falls upon the group much sooner than they would like, but with a full moon bright enough to cast shadows, they keep moving for another hour or more.

"We must stop and build a campfire so we can rest," Kang suggests strongly. "Besides we might miss seeing a trail in the dark."

"You are right. We need to stop," Ju agrees. "Start gathering twigs for a fire."

The group gathers twigs as night moves in the cool air. Hana snuggles close to Ju. It is a restless night for the group. Sleep doesn't come easily. The woods seem to come alive.

CHAPTER THIRTEEN

THE GROUP PRAYS

The next morning, everyone is ready to move, but where? Uneasy thoughts cause them not to want to take the lead or follow.

Ju reassures them. "We most likely have moved away from the trail in the dark. It may take us longer to find it. We will find it traveling east. Everyone, keep your eyes open for a hint of it."

"I have an idea," chirps Hana. "Let's ask the Father of Glory to help us find the right way to go. He can see everything we can't. I bet He can see the trail right now."

"You are right. He can see right through this whole jungle!" exclaims Kang.

"Oh glory hallelujah, now I have to live with two God walkers," groans Chang.

"You have said nothing this whole trip. And that's what comes out of your mouth?" snaps Ju. "I make number three."

"Count me in. I am number four. Do you have something to say about that?" challenges Shin.

Chang rolls his eyes.

"Today, Father, show my dad the trail, where it went to," begins Hana. "And help Chang to like you." And then she whispers, "I don't think he likes you."

Chang smiles to himself.

"Bring us a guide," adds Kang.

"An honest guide," amends Shin.

"And help us to get along," prays Kang.

"Protect all of us from all dangers." Ju yields to God.

"Make my daddy strong and smart," prays Hana.

"Hey, what about me?" Shin winks.

"And Shin."

Kang nods to her.

"And Kang," she adds. "Chang too."

"We should have done this yesterday," states Kang.

"I think we were all too frightened to speak," says Ju.

They start their journey with renewed hope in spite of the uncertainty of their steps. There is also the realization that each step is taking them farther away from being sent back to North Korea where certain death awaits them. As they walk, they become more aware of their surroundings. How beautiful it is! The sun shines through the thick roof of the trees and makes sunspots on the ground. They dance around in front of the travelers, making them wonder if fairies really do exist. The warmth of the day makes them feel at home, and the nature around them enfolds them like a blanket. They feel God's security. They stop only for lunch, not really certain how long they have been walking.

Suddenly, Hana, forgetting herself altogether, runs ahead of the group. They helplessly watch. As suddenly as she takes off in a full sprint, she seems to hit an invisible wall. Ju runs after her and has to keep himself from falling down into a hidden ravine.

Still standing in her fixed position, she turns toward her dad in amazement. "Angels," Hana states simply.

Ju is speechless.

"Angels must have stopped you," Kang says as she approaches and peers down into the gulf below. "Something stood in your way."

"I felt it."

Ju picks Hana up. "Hana, you could have been killed. Do not do that again."

"Yes, sir," she answers respectfully. "I am sorry. It will not happen again. I just feel so happy. I want to run."

After the group regains their bearings, they are forced to look at their newly discovered situation. They stand on top of a ridge. It gives them an aerial view of their surroundings. Stretching before them is a dense jungle and mountainous region.

"I think we need to sit down and observe what is before us," suggests Shin. They all stare without looking. Their minds begin to unravel from the shock of reality.

"That was amazing," Chang says as he looks below. "Something stopped you. You didn't teeter. What was it?"

Kang gives her brother *the look*. "What do you think?"

As Ju observes the vast unknown, he whispers, "Keep my thoughts clear, God. Give us direction."

Shin places his hand on Ju's shoulder. "You are not alone."

"Hey," says Hana, "you can yell as loud as you want!" She struggles out of her father's arms."

"You're right," Chang talks to his newfound friend.

"Have the contest over here, away from our 'guides,'" instructs Kang, sounding very much like a mom. She directs them away from Ju and Shin.

"Look," continues Ju. "See how the land falls over there and then flattens out? The trees almost curve around something."

"Like a ribbon?" adds Shin. "It's most likely a stream or a river. We do need water."

"Yes, we do," Ju adds, thinking, *And there should be a trail nearby a stream. Everyone needs water. But how do we get there? What we are standing on seems like a massive stadium with walls that jet straight down.*

"I think we will have to walk along the edge of this and travel South," advises Shin.

"What you say sounds logical to me." Ju accepts his idea.

The group begins walking, Ju taking the lead and Shin protecting from behind. It is dusk before they reach the tail of the cathedral and can begin to descend.

"We can't climb down in the dark," interjects Shin.

"I believe you are right," agrees Ju.

Everyone is exhausted, and they are all thankful they will rest for the night. They sleep another undirected night. This time, when they awake, they are a team. They are awakened to a purpose. Their bodies are rested, and their minds are alert. The distance is filled with boulders taller than they are. They have to read the rocks and choose a pathway. They help each other and hand Hana down when needed. It takes them all afternoon to get down to more solid ground The terrain is rocky but offers a few flat spaces of open ground. They are no longer able to see the stream. They have to use their sense of direction. They begin to travel east again. It isn't long before they find it. The water is a much-needed provision.

"He leads me beside still waters!" exclaims Hana. "He is leading us." She says it like when you lose sight of someone and then you find him or her again.

"We can't rest for long," exhorts Ju.

"We can walk beside it, can't we?" asks Kang.

"Yes, we can. It is traveling southeast, and we will come to the ocean or Thailand at some point." As they walk, Kang begins to sing a familiar song.

"The Lord shall guide you in dry places and make strong your bones. And you shall be like a watered garden." It is from Isaiah 58:11. As Kang sings this song, she teaches it to Hana. Chang joins in after a while, having known the song since childhood.

Hana and Kang hold hands, and secret tears flow down Ju's face, one by one. No one sees them, as he is walking ahead. They sing the song repeatedly. The song intensifies for Ju as he hears the familiar voice of Sun'hi. He has heard her hum the same song. He keenly feels her presence even though she is thousands of miles away. He is thinking, *Don't stop singing. I hear her voice.* They don't stop.

***

Thousands of miles away, Sun'hi sings, "You shall be like a spring of water whose waters fail not." The familiar song came to her mind as if it were passing through corridors. She hasn't sung the song in a very long time, certainly not since she left Korea. She is sitting on the park bench with her friend, Mi-ran. They watch her friend's son play on the playground. Sun'hi takes comfort in holding her friend's newborn.

"Are you singing?" asks Mi-ran.

"Yes, I am."

She continues singing. The baby coos at her. Mi-ran lays her head on Sun'hi's shoulder as they share the infant's gaze.

"I like listening to you sing. My mother used to sing to me," says Mi-ran.

Sun'hi's heart is wrapped in a closely guarded ray of hope hidden deep inside a locked treasure chest. Ever since Hana left with Ju about three months ago, Zhao Tao has also been gone. He is not expected to return for another three months. Runaway tears drop one by one as she sings the song repeatedly. She keenly senses Ju's presence, and she too does not want the moment to end.

***

"Look, Ju," says Chang. "Smoke."

Ju is awakened from his dream, and he is brought back to the woods. "What?" he answers, somewhat irritated.

"I didn't mean to disturb you, dreamboat, but look, smoke!"

Sure enough, there, a short distance away, he can see smoke from a village campfire. Everyone's steps quicken as the group draws nearer. At precisely the same time, they are discovered by the villagers, whose men have surrounded them from behind.

"Look it's a village!" states Chang with excitement. "How do we let them know we are here? And we need help? Like a guide?"

From behind them, they hear angry words that they do not understand. Turning around, they find themselves surrounded and confronted by a group of the village men. Ju speaks to them in Cantonese, which they do not understand. He tries Mandarin of which he only knows a few words. "Hello, we need your help."

"I think they speak Hmong," whispers Shin.

Speaking in their own language, they make gestures to the group to enter their village. The group is hesitant to follow, but they have no choice.

"Are they going to kill us?" asks Hana.

"No. No," answers Ju. "We have no weapons. We are not a threat to them. But we are strangers. We will have to try to gain their trust and help."

A villager makes a gesture that seems to mean "Come," and then to their surprise, he speaks one word in Mandarin: "Come."

The villagers lower their guns at the command of the man. Village children and women stand at the doors of their homes. The group is brought to the center of the village where there are baking ovens fueled with wood. There is a pleasant smell, which helps relax the group. The leader gestures to them to sit down. Again, Ju tries to speak.

"We are lost." He points to the southeast. "We are trying to get to Bangkok, Thailand."

The leader repeats, "Bangkok, Thailand?"

"Bangkok," repeats Ju.

The leader repeats the word to the villagers in their own language. Some women bring them rice cakes. The travelers bow their heads in gratitude before receiving the gift of food.

"I think I remember the words *lost* and *guide* in Hmong," Shin informs Ju. "I will try."

"Lost," says Shin.

The leader nods his head to indicate he understands.

"Guide?" He offers the leader some money. "Pay?"

One villager gets very excited. Speaking in his own language and with gestures, he pushes Shin's hand away. He returns to his nearby home and comes back, carrying in his arms a small child who is clearly sick with a raging fever. "He wants medicine not money." He turns to Ju.

Ju reaches into his backpack and pulls out a bottle that contains pills that are a fever reducer and a bottle containing an antibiotic. "I was saving this for an emergency. But I think I have enough to give him and still have enough for later use."

"I have the same in my backpack. We will be fine," Kang assures Ju. Kang gestures to the father to let her hold the child. She makes a sign for a drink. And the father complies. He hands the child to her and gets a glass of water. She begins to minister to the child. She carefully gets him to shallow the pills and prays for Jesus to heal the child. The villagers and the travelers watch with anticipation. Within a short time, the fever clearly subsides. The child begins to wake up and soon is looking into the face of the kind stranger. Quickly, the mother comes over and takes the child. Tears are running down her face. Kang attempts to explain to the parents how to administer the medicine. The father gestures to Ju by pointing southwest and then to himself. "Bangkok." He then holds up three fingers and points to the sun.

"I think we have our guide." He puts his hand on Ju's shoulder. "Yes, in three days. We need the rest." During the three-day stay, they treat a few other children who are sick. When they are ready to leave, they are given rice cakes to fill their backpacks. The travelers leave most of the medicine with the villagers and have the feeling they have done something to help save some young lives. Relieved and refreshed, the travelers leave with their guide. It is about a four-day journey through the woods, and they will have to cross another border. The journey to Thailand along the maze of trails, although beautiful, is uneventful. Every tree, rock, and stream looks the same. The border crossing is barely noticeable, as they cross in the middle of nowhere. There is no change until they are fairly close to Bangkok. This is where their guide hands them over to another guide who apparently has guided other refugees from Korea to the South Korean embassy. He is also able to speak some Korean and is a citizen of Thailand. Their guide from Laos is terribly eager to get back to his village. The good-byes are short.

Their new guide is evasive and more of a businessman. He demands money up front. Ju and the others comply, but Ju warns them not to reveal how much money they may actually have, reminding them they need to have money for their flight over to Korea from Thailand.

CHAPTER FOURTEEN

FREEDOM FIGHTERS

Once at the embassy, they are received but treated as a nuisance. They are transported to the international detention center of Bangkok. It is a training camp for North Koreans. They are given beds and a small living area. The travelers meet other North Koreans. Some have been hiding in China for years. Others, like Ju, have spent a very short time in China. Thailand makes no distinction between North and South Korea. They view them as one Korea. The Korean refuges must be trained in the ways of modern life before they are "deported" to South Korea. They need to be caught up to the twenty-first century. This helps to alleviate the culture shock. Some individuals have been at the camp longer than others. It all depends on whether they came with finances or have none.

At a camp meeting, they are invited to listen to a man address the recent arrivals. "You were brave to come here." The man encourages the group, "You are the true freedom fighters—and without guns. Your weapon is your willingness to leave. Each one of you has risked your life to leave. Why? If North Korea is so wonderful, why would you go to such great lengths to leave? The whole world wants to know. The world needs to be told the truth. The more freedom fighters who leave, the more you expose its atrocities and the more you weaken the North Korean regime. You, my friends, are courageous fighters."

After the speaker is done, he approaches their group. "I am an American. I believe you may have been guided by an American out of China into Laos."

"We were," answers Ju. "How did you know?"

"I didn't. But we have been asking all the new refugees. We want you to know he is safe. You are the last ones he was able to help. You have been a great concern for him. He was afraid that he had lost you. It will come to him as great news to hear you have safely arrived at this camp."

"Where is he?" asks Shin.

"He is in America and unable to return to China. They will not give him another visa and have banned him from the country. He has been helping freedom fighters to escape for years. He is great at what he does, but he was bound to get caught at some point."

"What happened to the others who were caught?" asks Hana.

"Little one, they were sent back to North Korea."

"To live?"

"No, to die. They are considered criminals. And their crime calls for the death penalty," the speaker says gravely.

"Or they will be sent to one of the gulags to die a slow death," answers Shin. There is silence in the group as they show respect for those who have left them. They feel astounded that they just made it through. It could have been them, and they feel ashamed.

"Please, do not feel ashamed. You must feel blessed, and you have lived for them," consoles the speaker.

"How?" asks Kang.

"You where brave enough to not give up. You supported each other through the mountains and jungles of Laos. Your lives testify to the urgency of stopping North Korea. Your coming will help save other lives. And who knows? Maybe they will be given another opportunity to escape. It has happened before," he assures the travelers.

The next day, the process to acclimate them begins. Hana picks up on things faster than the others. They are taught how to use a computer, how to use a bank card, and so on. They are questioned regarding what vocation they might pursue. Ju expresses an interest in radio. As the days progress, they see less and less of their fellow travelers. Ju and Hana are going to leave sooner. This is mainly because of the position Ju held in North Korea. Even though he did not have a position of authority, he had had close contact with Kim Jung Eun. Officials in South Korea want to talk to him extensively. He may have information that may help South Korea.

When it comes time for them to leave, Hana wants to say good-bye to their fellow travelers.

"Don't worry about us, Hana," Kang reassures her. "We will leave here at the right time. But right now we need to care for the people here. We need to encourage them. We may leave for America."

"America?" asks Hana.

"Yes, they have colleges that Chang and I would like to attend. We would make a new home there," Kang says excitedly.

"I will never see you again!" cries Hana. "Good-bye. Good-bye." She hugs their necks.

***

Once on the airplane, Ju feels very nervous. He calms himself down by talking to Hana, who is chattering away about her new school. She wonders if she will make friends. The plane lands, and Ju and Hana's feet touch Korean soil for the first time in months. This Korea is free. They are escorted to a waiting cab where they are given a ride to an apartment center designed for North Koreans who need to adjust. The ride to their new home is overwhelming—the lights, the colors, the cars. Everywhere they look, people are dressed differently, wearing what they wish, walking where they wish. They pass a church and look in wonder. Hundreds of people are standing outside or walking into the building, unafraid. They don't hide it. They have Bibles in their hands.

"Look, Daddy! Those people have their own Bibles. They don't care if someone sees them. Look! Even little girls carry them in their hands!"

They see a Buddhist temple. They see the same thing; people are free to walk in and out. They don't have to hide who they are. The man who is driving them came from a ministry center called *Hanawou*; it is a settlement support center. He is enjoying their wonder and interjects, "I love to hear people who come here and see with their own eyes for the first time freedom. It is like seeing things with new eyes. You will be staying in an apartment set up by our ministry. You will both start classes on Monday, tomorrow. If you wish, you can attend church with us tonight. If you are too tired, rest. It is your choice.

Choice? thought Ju. *I can choose?*

"I want to go! I want to go!" exclaims Hana.

Ju smiles. "Maybe I don't have a choice after all. We will go," answers Ju.

It is wonderful. The people at the church greet them with much excitement. They welcome them like they are their own brothers and sisters. People at the church sing loudly and with much enthusiasm. Hana is given her own Bible.

She grins. "If only my mom could see me now." She turns the pages and finds children's pictures. "Hey, I need to learn how to read better."

"You start school tomorrow. And your Daddy will start a school that will give him job skills."

"I really love this country."

Ju is suddenly overwhelmed by how safe he feels—and more than that, how safe Hana is at that moment. Waves of overwhelming gratitude flood his being.

The next day, Hana is taken to school.

"A military official is going to talk to you today about whatever you might know," their host informs them. "Don't be afraid. Your information may only confirm information they already have."

Hana thinks being dropped off at school is great. Knowing she will see her dad at the end of the day makes her feel independent. There are a few students like her. The teachers are impressed by how well she can read already.

"Most children like you have had no chance to learn."

Hana is different.

A little girl is assigned to her to take her to her classroom and to lunch. She is slightly older than Hana.

"Hi, Hana. My name is Kim Chun-ee. I am here to help you for the next couple of weeks. Do you like school?" her new friend inquires.

"I don't know," answers Hana. "I have never been to a school before. I am only six. I have already started to read. My dad taught me."

"Really! Did your mom teach you anything?" she asks with interest.

"Well, she taught me some songs and poems and about Jesus, but she couldn't come with us. She had to stay back in China," Hana says sadly.

"China? Why China? Isn't she Korean like you and your dad?" Chun-ee is confused.

"Yes, she is, but she was sold as a bride to her husband the night she was supposed to marry my dad. Well, he became my dad once he learned about me and I needed him to help me. My real dad is Chinese. He would hate me if he knew I was a girl. So, my mom hid me as a boy," Hana explains.

"What do you mean?" Chun-ee is trying to understand.

"I had to pretend I was a boy most of my life." And then Hana changes directions. "I really miss my mom. My daddy is going to find her and bring her here."

"How is he going to do that?" Chun-ee asks doubtfully.

"I don't know," says Hana, knowing she speaks the impossible truth.

***

Chun-ee thinks about what Hana has told her. When she returns home that night, she tells her father about Ju and Hana. Her father is intrigued by the story and wants to meet Ju and Hana. They meet at the steps of the school the next day.

CHAPTER FIFTEEN

THE GROOM SENDS FOR HIS BRIDE

"Sir, my name is Kim Seong-min. Your name is Ju?" Chun-ee's father introduces himself.

"Yes. How did you know?" he asks, puzzled by the knowledge of this stranger.

"My daughter has made friends with your daughter. I will get right to the point. I hear Hana's mother is living in northern China. I visit this area frequently on business for my company." He pauses and continues, "I know of someone who has a relative in the town she lives in. He is a good friend. I would like to try to help." He waits again for Ju's response. "Is Hana's mother your wife?"

"No, sir. Sun'hi was my fiancée. I don't know how I can bring her home to us." Ju closes his eyes and then opens them, looking upward. "I believe she will be my bride again." He speaks with undying hope.

"That makes you the groom." Kim Seong-min smiles at his newfound friend.

Ju's love for Sun'hi compels him to make an unthinkable request of this stranger. "I have a little money I can give you. Could you bring her home to me? To Hana?" asks Ju, knowing he has no right to ask.

"I would like very much to bring her home," Seong-min assures him.

"How soon can you go?" Ju is unable to wait.

"Within the next week or two. I need to know the exact location and the residence if possible," says Seong-Min.

"I know all of this. I will help any way I can." Ju's confidence is building. "I could go with you?"

"No, you must stay here." Seong-Min puts his hand on his newfound friend's shoulder. "You must be brave enough to stay here."

Ju places both of his hands on Seong-Min's shoulder. Looking into Seong-Min's eyes, he holds his gaze intently.

"You must not fail. You must bring her home to me." Ju's passion for his bride is gripping. "You must go and bring her back to me as if you were me. Nothing less will suffice."

In this moment, Seong-Min becomes bonded to this young man's passion. A silent understanding is transferred to him. He is now a servant to a mission, Ju's mission.

"I have something you must take with you that will that let her know without a doubt that it is me who wants to bring her here," Ju instructs. "I have a picture of this flower. A doraji."

"A doraji?" Seong-Min acknowledges the groom's words.

"This flower represents hope to her and our love. It will let her know it is me." Ju is almost breathless. "Oh, I hope you can go quickly." He pauses, looking down as he thinks about the possible danger. "You may be able to get there before her husband comes back. He spends months in Russia working in the lumber industry; that is where I met him," Ju explains. "Sun'hi's sole purpose for him is to produce sons or at least one. He does not love her." His words race on. "Sun'hi has convinced him that Hana is a boy. Her first daughter she gave birth to he destroyed on the day she was born." He closes his eyes contemplating what could have happened to their Hana. "Who knows what would have happened if he had discovered Hana was not a son?"

The more Ju thinks about it, the more he feels the urgency of bringing her here to him. Zhao Tao could decide she is useless to him and send her back to North Korea or he could sell her to sex traffickers. "You must go soon. God must be protecting her. It must be why we have made it here so quickly." Ju pushes on Kim Seong-min's shoulders, which are still within his grip.

Kim Seong-min puts his hands on Ju's shoulder with equal intensity. "Ju, God is protecting her. She will be safe. I'll move my appointments around to make my departure sooner. As you have instructed me, I will go in your stead and not fail you. I will call you soon."

Ju could not concentrate at his new job at the radio station.

"Pay attention, or go home. Do you really want this job?" his boss yells at him.

Ju does everything he can to keep on task. Luckily that evening, Ju receives a phone call. It is from Kim Seong-min.

"I leave tomorrow. I'll come and get the picture of the flower tonight," he informs Ju.

"I'll be ready." Ju hangs the phone up. He looks up at the moon. "Sun'hi, I am coming for you, just like I promised." Ju feels weak inside. "A promise, a promise I cannot keep. Nothing is happening that I can make happen, plans for all of this are …" He quietly sits down as he feels power from the Father of Glory. He feels the pores of his being drink Him in. Hope touches him and strengthens him, every part of him. Words cannot be spoken, for they do not exist. A symphony of love plans each note that creates a song that no one can sing. It has not been sung before, until now.

***

Kim Seong-min starts his journey to bring Sun'hi back for Ju. He has the flower, which will be the code he needs to help her understand that he can be trusted. He has the money needed to buy the bride for the groom. He rarely rescues refugees from North Korea. He limits his rescue attempts to protect his identity and not bring attention to himself. He does not want to jeopardize his business contacts or the lives of those he is rescuing. China will often look the other way if the climate is right. He talks to himself, "The political climate that is." Right now, the climate seems fair.

This mission is different. He has been commissioned by a young man and is going in his place. He feels a certain urgency. He decides not to take detours, linger at hotels, or get into long lunch and dinner conversations. The winter has been unusually warm, which means the logging in Russia might possibly be slowed down—for a short time.

Kim Seong-min reaches Fu Yuan and meets the business contacts he has in the area. The area produces rice in the late spring, and his company trades with them. The meeting is brief. After the meeting, he asks for directions to the only park in town. He plans to inquire for directions to her home from those at the park.

At his arrival, there are a few women with their children playing at the park. For him to approach them would raise suspicion. He decides to walk around the park so as to portray himself as a businessman out for a walk. He is listening to their conversations. He knows he is not on this rescue alone and is attentive to the impossible happening. At this very moment, he hears a young mother call another woman "Sun'hi." This is a common name; however, he decides he will approach the women and speak in Mandarin, asking them if they have ever seen a flower like the one in the picture he shows them.

Sun'hi's looks at the picture he shows them. Her eyes do not betray her astonishment. She answers casually, "Yes, sir, they grow in this park by the stream."

"Would you be kind enough to show an old man where they grow?" Seong-min inquires.

"Yes, I could show you; it is not far." She nods to her friend. "I'll be right back."

"Sun'hi, be careful." Mi-ran speaks to her in Korean. "The one thing that is worse than being in a forced marriage is being taken to a brothel." Married women, especially Korean women, are viewed as a product that can be bought and sold or stolen. There are no laws to protect them, as they live in China illegally. The only person who can truly protect them is their husband. Sun'hi has not seen her husband since he left for the logging camp in the hopes of retrieving his son.

As Sun'hi walks beside this stranger, she stays in plain sight of her friend Mi-ran so as not to alarm her. She bends down to show him where the flowers grow. She knows they do not grow here in this place. The only people who know about this flower are her daughter and Ju. She glances in the stranger's eyes. He speaks. "Are you Hana's mother?"

She nods yes.

"Ju has sent me here to bring you to him in South Korea." He carefully pauses to let her soak this information in. "Will you come with me? I must leave within the hour."

She nods as he bows. She thinks about what she might need and then realizes there is nothing in her home she needs or wants. "I can leave now," she answers.

"I need you to meet me at the train station," he instructs her.

"There is a market there. I will wait at the flower stand," she responds.

"I will walk by you, and you can follow me to the station entrance. I will have a ticket for you."

Sun'hi returns to Mi-ran. "He only wanted to see where the flower grew. I don't think he meant any harm," she tells her friend.

"All the same, I will walk you home," she assures her friend.

"I'll be fine. I am planning to go to the market." She brushes her friend off.

"Today?" Mi-ran thinks her friend is acting peculiarly.

"I forgot to buy some ginger for my meal. Did you hear our husbands may be returning soon? I was going to be ready for him," she explains herself.

"When he returns, maybe you will become pregnant again and have another son that will not be stolen from you," Mi-ran encourages her friend.

"You are so good to me, Mi-ran." Sun'hi says her farewell.

Mi-ran pauses. "Are you okay?"

"I am fine. I'll see you back in the neighborhood in about a half an hour. I'll come get the recipe you used to make. I will also buy a piece of candy from the market for your son." She keeps herself from saying more. *Maybe when I said, "You are so good to me," I was telling her good-bye in my own way.* She whispers a silent good-bye to Mi-ran. "Mi-ran, you are my good friend, and I will never forget you."

Once at the market, Sun'hi waits. She buys the ginger and a lollipop for Mi-ran's son. She waits near the flower stand, looking carefully at each flower. This is not unusual for her to do. However, she feels she cannot linger any longer and decides to return home. The decision is too depressing, and she knows she just can't return. It will mean returning to hopelessness. She dismisses her thoughts when she finally catches a glimpse of the man who had approached her at the park. She begins to follow him from a safe distance. She hopes he has seen her. He has given her no recognition with his eyes. The fear in her escalates as she crosses the threshold of the market into the area of the train station. Suddenly, she hears her name.

"Sun'hi!" It is her husband, Zhao Tao. She bows her head out of respect but also to hide her face because of the fear and disappointment she may reveal. She begins to feel herself shake.

"What are you doing here?" he inquires.

"I am buying ginger for dinner." All of a sudden, she trips, spilling the ginger on the ground along with the package of lollipops she just bought for Mi-ran's son.

Kim Seong-min can see what is happening and thinks quickly. He approaches Zhao Tao with confidence.

"I am Kim Seong-min, and I am here on a business trip."

"Who are you?" Zhao Tao is uncomfortable.

"I am a businessman and couldn't help notice this woman must be useless to you. I've watched her drop the food she has just now purchased. I buy unwanted women. Would you perhaps be interested in selling her to me?"

Zhao Tao was startled by the man's bold approach. "I just returned home. I don't know yet if she is useless to me."

"I am offering you two hundred yen." It is more than the price he had paid for her about seven years ago.

"Let me think about it. Will you be here tomorrow?"

"The deal holds right now. If you don't want it, I can go somewhere else. What will it be? Yes or no."

Sun'hi keeps her head down during this transaction. She begins to shake almost uncontrollably.

"What is wrong with you, Sun'hi?" Zhao Tao demands. "I believe this man is right; you have been useless to me. I don't need to think about it. He turns to the man. "I will take your offer."

Kim Seong-min hands Zhao Tao the money. He grabs Sun'hi roughly. She begins to cry from the anxiety, helplessness, and hopelessness.

She wonders, *Is this man really going to take me to my Hana and to Ju?*

By now, she is confused. But it is truly out of her hands. She has just been bought and sold. Kim Seong-min sounds so real she wonders if she herself has been tricked. Kim Seong-min shakes her hard and tells her to shut up. He tells her in a loud, hard voice so Zhao Tao can hear him.

"Now you are mine, and you will stop, or I'll send you back to North Korea."

Sun'hi manages to stop crying and boards the train. They ride the train until they make a switch to another train. At the next stop, He calmly reassures her. "Sun'hi, I am glad you resisted me. It helped your husband to sell you to me."

"I haven't seen him in months, and just now he shows up. I was afraid, and then you scared me."

'It's all right now, Sun'hi. I am taking you to Ju and your daughter. From here on out, you are to pose as my daughter. Your name is Kim Su-jin. I have a passport for you with that name. We will fly to South Korea tomorrow morning." Tomorrow. She is afraid to fall asleep for fear it is all a dream or she may never wake up. And when she wakes up, it will all be gone. She is afraid to hope. She is afraid that somehow unknown forces will know she is escaping to safety and to love and put a stop to it. If she doesn't think, no one will know she exists. "Maybe I can hold my breath."

In the morning, Kim Seong-min holds her hand as they walk to the taxi from the hotel and then from the taxi to the airport and then the airport terminal onto the plane. He stands behind her with his hands on her shoulders. She feels blind, as if she is peering down a dark tunnel with light at the end a long way off. She realizes she is being guided along. Is it Kim Seong-min holding her hand? She knows whose hand she holds. She knows whose voice she follows; it is not a stranger's voice. She will not be able to follow. She can follow because it is not the voice of a stranger. He is her eyes. He is the one who forges the pathway that is in front of her. His steps are before her. She is about ready to enter the plane. Her eyes are open as she takes in all that surrounds her. She is safe. She has always been safe. But nothing can steal this freedom from her. Freedom. What does that mean? Can you understand the meaning of a word you have not experienced? Can the experience you are having have a word for it? All she knows is she is safe, safe to smile, safe to have her own thoughts. The large glass windows of the airport overlook the ocean.

The sun is beginning to rise. The glow and colors in the sky illuminate the world around them. She can see all the world around her. The sun comes into full view. Its brilliance reflects in the ocean. Its glory seems to circle them and explode. Sun'hi feels she can do the same, explode with light. She is overcome with joy and laughter. Before they enter, they have to pass through the security gates. Kim Seong-min is being questioned.

Sun'hi hears the words. "He is not your father as your passport claims, is he?" They continue to interrogate her. "You have been bought and sold, haven't you?"

The words sound far away, distant as if they are being whispered through a long, dark tunnel. She does not answer their questions.

"You do not have to be sold to this man. We are going to send you back to your homeland, North Korea."

"I thought that is where I was headed." Sun' hi finds her voice. She finds herself being stolen back. How can she be stolen back?

The moment, the time, the desire is being stolen, stolen back away from her—her freedom, her Ju, her Hana. She is being led away from freedom as if it were the enemy. But it is the enemy leading her to a place of death. Kim Seong-min is helpless, as he is in danger of being arrested. Instead, he is stripped of his passport and placed on the plane to South Korea. Only moments and Sun'hi would have been on this very plane with Kim Seong-min. He will have to return empty-handed. Sun'hi is deported back to her country of birth.

She wonders if the only reason for her life is death.

CHAPTER SIXTEEN

IN HER HOMELAND, JUNGEORI

Once back in her homeland, she is given the chance by her government to learn her real purpose in life. She is given this opportunity for having "left." She is sent to Jungeori. She is given a uniform specially made for those working in the fields. Sun'hi closes her eyes as her hands touch the dry earth. She lets the dust run though her hands. She has been given a small rake to break the dirt up for planting soybeans. She works beside hundreds of others all given the same opportunity by their generous government. As she works on this day, which could be her first day or two-thousandth day, she watches a breathtaking sight. A young man successfully catches a rat. He breaks its neck quietly and conceals it cleverly in his clothing. She can't imagine what he is saving it for. She works the rest of the day without a break.

At the end of the day, unknown to him, she manages to follow him. He is not found out by the guards either. He skins the rat with a sharp stone and eats it raw. She almost gags at the sight. It is then he notices her. He makes eye contact with her. She wonders if she is looking into the eyes of a human being. He turns away from her in fear of her trying to take it away from him. He snarls at her in warning.

As she looks away, she looks up at the surrounding mountains. The night air falls quickly and with it the temperature. She shivers. She follows the others to her sleeping quarters. However, before they get there, she is given a small cup of soybeans and corn, which have been carefully counted so everyone receives the same amount. Tonight, they are being given a special treat for having worked so hard. They get to hear the rules of the camp and have the chance to recite them before going to bed. Her sleeping area is small, and she has very little room to stretch. She sleeps curled up. The only thing that helps her sleep is exhaustion. The only thing that gives her breath is knowing Hana is not with her and safe with Ju. Hana lives. But how will Hana awaken?

When Sun'hi wakes up, she is unable to remember how long she has been there. She really wants to stay asleep. One moment is like the next moment in Jungeori, a gulag or labor camp. One hour is like the next hour. One day is like the next day. One month is like the next month. One year is like the next year. Each day she views a new horror.

Are some people really not human? she wonders. *Maybe I am not …* She pauses in her thoughts. "… human."

She wakes to go to the field to work. On her way, she sees others so thin they are bent over. Their backs can no longer stand straight. She returns to her bed at the end of the day. One day on the way to the fields, she sees a young girl taken from their labor group and a guard openly accuse her. She pleads to no avail. He chooses to rape her in front of "nonidentities."

Who is the animal now? Sun'hi wonders in disgust.

The girl is left naked in her shame a reminder to her she is worthless. Later on that endless day, Sun'hi is gathered with other field hands to watch the executions. Men—they are so deformed from malnutrition and disease that it is difficult to ascertain their human form—are tied to trees ready to be shot. She stands looking at her feet. She pushes the dirt with her feet in a half circle. She forces herself to look up as required. She looks though the sight before her and to the mountains. There they stand towering over this atrocity.

I thought they were meant to protect us. She observes their height and grandeur. Their presence is intimidating. *But all they do is conceal us. The mountains are disconnected from what takes place before them. How dare they invite our eyes to behold them in their beauty?* Sun'hi directs her anger toward the nature around her. It almost seems callous with all the horror around them. She thinks about the mountains as having a soul. *They have no voice and therefore do not speak,* she reasons. *They have no brain so therefore they do not think. They just exist.*

Sun'hi feels the same. She only exists, and she looks down at her feet, moving the dirt back and forth in a circular motion. She hears the gunshots, and the subhumans stop breathing. Their bodies are thrown into graves dug by their own hands. The nonidentities' presences are no longer required, and they are dismissed.

How does the human spirit live through hell on earth with no hope of leaving? It must be something God gives not just to animals but to humans as well, an instinct to survive.

Survival for what? Sun'hi's purpose for life is being purged. Her tainted blood has been removed from society so as not to infect it. Maybe she will be cleansed and returned to the community.

Something lies in her heart concealed, similar to the young man who drew away from her when he hid the rat. Hope. Hope and value. He believes his life has value. Why else would he attempt to keep himself alive? Hope and value are stirring in her heart. She knows in her heart she is not tainted; she has value. It is this very morning she notices someone, the girl who had been raped. She is pregnant. Most people would not notice. But Sun'hi does notice. Life is stirring in this young girl. And Sun'hi feels life stir in her inner being. She becomes aware of Christ within her and among her. She senses His glory, which overwhelms her to the point she thinks surely she has left this world and must be in heaven. Alas it is not time. She wants to help this young girl live. She begins to make plans. She looks for an opportunity to find extra food to give to the girl, whether in the fields or the rations given out. She looks for ways to receive more food to give away. She is not the only one helping this girl. There are others who are helping her. It is an unspoken revolution. Fear is being displaced by compassion. With each passing day, Camp Jungeori becomes more of a shadow to her and the ever-present kingdom of the Father of Glory the reality. This reality is a gift to her. She starts to think she sees Him with her, walking by her during the day. She releases it to the other people living with her. They may need an act of kindness. She looks for Him in their need—lending help when someone feels weaker, offering a song to her creator, playing a game with small children, telling them a story, praying with someone before his or her execution, noticing when the sun is shining and the sky is blue. This is what lifts her up above survival to the purpose.

Feeding this young woman is a crime. Sun'hi has to be careful. She just can't walk up to the girl and hand her extra food. She has to plan. Sometimes she makes sure she is right in front of her in the fields and leaves her a gift of food in her pathway. She may pass her by when walking to or from somewhere and accidently bump into her. Or she might drop the food into her plate when passing by in the camp dining hall. This mission causes her to think through and be aware of her surroundings. She has to be extra careful of those who catch rats to eat. They are the most likely to tell on other inmates. They are in the camp only for their own survival and will do so by any means made available to them. This girl's pregnancy is a crime. In a few months, the young girl begins to show.

One of the rat-eating inmates exposes her secret. She has been discovered, and she is dragged to the execution site. She is tied to the tree, and all the women in the camp are forced to watch. The unborn baby is viciously cut from her uterus and suffocated before her eyes. She is left to bleed to death. The bystanders are forced to watch until she breathes her last. Sun'hi is in shock. She feels the breath leave her. She does not move but stares blankly. Tears roll down her cheek. She is strangely thankful for each one. She can feel the young girl's value and the baby's value, her own value. She may not have known her name. She may have not spoken with her voice. Her actions are her voice. She, the young girl, and the baby are human.

Is there more to say? Did it change anything? Did Sun'hi stop looking for needs? The story continues. You can begin again when Sun'hi first came; the story just repeats itself. The whole world silently watches like the mountains with no voice. The world does not do what it is meant to do, protect. The world conceals what it knows. It does not think and therefore does not speak. The world just exists.

But then …

CHAPTER SEVENTEEN

BUT THEN SOMETHING DOES HAPPEN

How news reaches Jungeori is a mystery. Information coming in or out is carefully guarded. It was heard that eighty souls had been marched to an undisclosed stadium. The stadium had been filled with citizens to witness the executions of these souls. Even though executions are a daily part of life at the gulag, eighty was unheard of, especially in a public place such as a stadium.

On this very day, Sun'hi is being released back into society. She has served her sentence for having left the country. Also, a rumor has circulated that one thousand souls will be marched out of a gulag to a stadium where again citizens of the country will be forced to watch. Sun'hi is one of ten thousand who will be forced to watch.

As she sits in the stadium with thousands of others, she wonders what they think. She looks upon those who are about to face execution. One of them could have been her. Maybe this is why she is given a seat closer to the front. Her vision clears, and she able to see individuals. Some, she notices, are in family groups. Moms and dads hold their little ones close to their sides. Very old men stand alone. Most of them look barely human. Suddenly she sees a young girl who is visibly pregnant. She stops breathing. She is not thinking of anyone else, herself included.

She runs down the aisle, passing unsuspecting guards and onto the field. She runs to this young girl and embraces her. It is as if no one else exists. And then she turns to face her executioners. Looking at the spectators, she realizes they are silent and time seems frozen and without movement. Her brave act speaks like thunder and clears the vision of the ten thousand. They too no longer see the masses but individuals. Human dignity and compassion overtake fear. They keenly sense their own individuality and that of those who face a firing squad. So very many face the firing squad. Something is breaking inside the people. The leader has gone too far and has broken though a barrier of intolerance.

Another individual runs down onto the field to shield a victim. Then ten run down and then a hundred and then one thousand. There is no stopping this wildfire. It is burning fear and releasing compassion. This fire laps at the feet of the soldiers. An unheard of sound begins to fill the stadium as hundreds of guards lock their weapons and lay them down as they too run onto the field. There are now more people on the field than in the seats.

Kim Jung Eun is left helpless. His insane commands are spoken but not heeded. He is powerless. And he is led out of the stadium. While this is going on, young people have been recording this event on their black-market cell phones. Sun'hi's unprecedented act has gone viral, as have the acts of the masses.

***

Someone is sleeping. Awaken, Hana. Hana opens her eyes and witnesses the event unfold in front of her eyes.

"Daddy!" she yells.

It causes him to jump out of his seat.

"Don't scare me like that!" he scolds her. "What do you want?"

"Look, Daddy! Look!" She hands him her iPad. At first, he does not see. "It is Mom."

He looks, and then he sees. He sees his Sun'hi. "Sun'hi," he whispers to her as if she can hear him. Such hope fills his being he cannot contain it.

"Daddy, look!" It is a podcast showing people running to the DMZ{Korean demilitarized zone at the 38th parallel} and attempting to tear it down. "Look! A bulldozer is ramming into the fence. No one is stopping them. People are pouring into the DMZ."

It is truly an amazing sight as the inconceivable and frightening miracle unfolds before them. It paralyzes Ju.

"Daddy, we must go! We must go find my mom!" She tugs on her father's arm, but he seems to have left this world. "Daddy!" She shakes him with her voice. "Let's go!"

Ju looks at her as if he is trying to wake up from a deep sleep. As soon as he does, he jumps from his seat, and with his daughter in tow, he runs outside to seek a way to the part of the DMZ barrier that is being torn down. Outside, they discover they are not the only ones who have this desire. Horns are honking, church bells are ringing, and women have put on their traditional *hanbok* and are drumming in unison. He quickly retrieves his car and begins driving north. It is not hard to do, as the traffic is flowing in that direction. The movie marquees are repeatedly replaying the scene where Sun'hi stands in front of the pregnant girl to shield her. Seeing the huge picture, Ju is certain it is her. He turns on the radio, which is continuously reporting the action that is taking place at the DMZ. It seems as if thousands are pouring into the forbidden wilderness. Ju is keeping his ears open to any location mentioned. Luckily, he already lives on the outskirts of the north side of Seoul. And he doesn't get caught in the growing traffic jam. Having visited the DMZ often gives him an advantage in knowing which roads to use to get to where people are crossing. On those previous visits, he would stare across the fortified area and pray. *But now*, he thinks, *I can cross not just with my words*. He doesn't allow the thoughts that try to enter the back of his mind about the impossibility of finding Sun'hi. All he knows is he has to start crossing. Ju parks the car and witnesses firsthand the destruction of the fence and barriers designed to keep people from crossing. They stood for well over sixty years. He holds Hana's hand as they walk toward the miracle. They are afraid at first, but confidence builds with each step. Their pace quickens the closer they come until they are running. They stop short as Hana takes her first step toward North Korea, as does Ju. They gasp for air as their breath is taken away by the gravity of the moment.

On the other side of the DMZ at the same moment, Sun'hi's feet also touch the soil of the forbidden wilderness. The sense of freedom is overwhelming. Her heroic act was followed by thousands of other individuals' heroic acts. She was carried around the stadium and celebrated as a hero. A huge crowd of individuals began marching to the DMZ. The plan was to march until they reached their destination. The North Korean soldiers who were on duty were not caught up in the excitement and stopped the oncoming group. There were not many, as it was a remote area of the DMZ. However, it wasn't long before they were given the orders to lay down their guns and if need be to help tear down the structure. It did not take much.

At first, the ground beneath her feet feels heavy and as if it is holding them in place, but with each passing step, it feels lighter until the air seems to carry her over the ground. It is then she sees a most incredible sight—thousands of dorajis are in full bloom, blanketing the floor of a field stretching for what seems to be miles. The purple, blue, and white balloons sway in the wind. She follows the floral pathway, as do Ju and Hana.

"Look, Daddy!" Hana exclaims. "Mama's flowers! They must be showing us the pathway to her."

Ju answers, "I believe you are right."

Their steps quicken, and they seem to follow the pathway leading them to where they need to go. The flowers are beautiful and grow unhindered, for man's presence has not interfered. Their steps quicken as the anticipation of not finding her is more real. It would be a fairy tale if they found her. Sometimes love does seem like a fairy tale that only happened thousands of years ago in places that have no names.

"Daddy, don't give up," Hana says as she feels her father's pace slow to a dead stop.

"Hana, we can't find her." He stops. "Maybe we were wrong. Maybe that wasn't her we saw." He looks around him. "This place is too big."

"Don't say that!" Hana flashes back at her father's words. She turns to face him. It is then she sees her mother in the distance behind them. They had passed each other.

"There she is, Daddy. There she is!"

He turns around, looking behind him. There in the far distance is a woman. She is so far away it could be any woman. He calls out to her. "Sun'hi! *Sun'hi!*" He yells louder the second time. Against his better judgment, he begins running toward her. "Sun'hi, Sun'hi!" He continues to yell as he runs with Hana close behind.

"Come back, Mama!" Hana yells. "Come back!"

Ju repeats what Hana is yelling, "Come back!"

Sun'hi stops and turns but is frightened by the sight of a man running toward her. She turns away and starts running the other way. Ju can see her running away and stops running. Hana runs ahead of him, forcing him to follow.

Out of the corner of her eye, Sun'hi sees the small child and realizes it must be Hana.

"Hana!" she gasps. "My little girl!" And she realizes the man is Ju. "Ju!" She is relieved. "Ju," she says with deep affection. She turns around and runs back toward them. "Hana! Ju!" she yells as she runs.

Ju, in his excitement, runs ahead of Hana. Sun'hi jumps into Ju's arms. He spins her around and sets her down. He takes her hands into his. Their eyes meet. They feel the rotation of the earth beneath their feet. Or is it Hana running around them in circles? For a moment, Sun'hi looks down at her feet.

With one hand, he lifts her chin gently so she can meet his gaze. He places his hand on her cheek, wanting to remove all the pain. His other hand, as if in a dance, holds her other soft cheek. They see past the pain. They see each other's dreams, hopes, and passion. He kisses her gently, pressing into the hope, into the dreams, and then deeply into their passion.

Hana continues to dance around them, spinning and jumping. She belongs to this embrace. Ju picks her up and places her into Sun'hi's waiting arms. Hana wraps her arms around her mother's neck, and her legs around her waist. Sun'hi embraces her daughter and whispers into her ear, "I love you, Hana. I will never let you go."

Ju holds them both. In the center of the thirty-eighth parallel, Ju speaks these words, "Hana, Hana, Hana, you are our one. You make us one."

Her name resonates throughout the whole earth in the hearts of all humankind.

Hana, come to the chosen.
Hana, come to the whole earth.
Awaken, Hana.

Edwards Brothers Malloy
Thorofare, NJ USA
January 4, 2016